CASTOR

VALLEY

LAW & ORDER SERIES

By

Graysen Morgen

2017

Acknowledgements

Special thanks to my editor, Megan Brady, who wasn't a fan of westerns until she began working in this series! *Muchas gracias!*

Dedication

For my wife.

ONE

Boone Creek, Colorado Territory

Late October 1882

The sun began to slowly drift behind Boone Mountain, gradually casting a shadow over the nearby, small town of Boone Creek. The lamplighters worked at a steady pace, climbing up ladders to light each of the kerosene powered lights that lined the streets.

A cool breeze blew, and Jessie Henry smiled at her wife, Ellie, tugging her a little closer as they strolled along, arm in arm, walking through town after having had dinner at the Kettle Kitchen. As the Town Marshal, Jessie made it a point to see every inch of town daily and be seen at the same time. She wanted to know what was going on, and truly believed her presence alone helped thwart unlawful activity. It had been just over a year since the horrifying shot that had nearly taken her life in a shootout with the McNally Brothers, a dangerous outlaw gang. Her recovery had lasted about a month, and all that remained was a small scar on her lower left side.

"I love it when the cold weather comes. The air is so crisp and clean," Ellie said excitedly.

"The snow turns everything into a slushy mess," Jessie replied, wrinkling her upper lip as she scanned the sidewalks, casually tipping her hat in a slight nod to the people milling about.

"Yes, but so does the rain…" Ellie paused. "I heard the house at the end of town is for sale. I believe it's the one right up here," she finished as they came upon it.

"I thought that was a rental house?" Jessie replied, looking at the small, cottage-style home. It was similar to the row of houses on the other end of town where Bert, her deputy marshal, lived with his wife Molly and their child, except this house had a short, picket fence around it.

"It was, but I guess Mayor Montgomery decided to sell it."

"He owns it?" Jessie asked.

"I think so. Molly said he owns a lot of the rental properties in town."

"How do I not know this?"

Ellie laughed. "You probably spend all of your time talking law stuff with him, not business."

"That's true," Jessie said as they turned and headed back down Main Street. "Do you…want a house?" she asked.

"I don't know. The room above the store has been my home since I moved here over four years ago, but the idea of having a house with an actual bedroom, and a real kitchen, and a separate sitting area does sound quite nice."

Jessie nodded.

"I mean, I know it's just the two of us, so we don't really need a whole lot of space, but…it would be nice to have a house. Maybe one day," she mumbled, trailing off.

"Good evening, Marshal Henry, Mrs. Henry," Pastor Noah said as he walked up to them.

"What brings you to this end of town?" Jessie asked, knowing he didn't go far from the church.

"Oh, Doc Vernon gave me some salve for my shoulder. The cold weather is barely starting to arrive, and it's already giving me a fit. Call it old age," he sighed. "What brings you two out and about? You thinking of buying the old Rayburn House?"

"Oh, no," Ellie answered, shaking her head. "I decided to accompany Jessie on her evening stroll before heading in for the night. We just had a lovely dinner over at the Kettle Kitchen."

"Who are the Rayburn's?" Jessie asked.

"Dove and Ethel Rayburn built that house. They were some of the first residents in Boone Creek. In fact, they were the original owners of the General Trade, back before your..."

"Deceased husband?" Ellie added with a wink.

"Yes...Mr. Fray. Anyway, they packed up one day and headed back east. Sold everything off on their way out."

"So, that's how Corny was able to get the store," Ellie whispered. She hadn't been privy to the deal, but Corny had acted like they'd struck it rich. *Too bad he hadn't had the sense to get the house in the deal.*

"Oh, yes. He got a great deal from what I heard."

"What about the house?"

"They sold it to the town, and it became a rental house. A lot of Boone Creek's revenue comes from rental houses. I believe the town owns all of them."

"How the hell did I not know any of this?" Jessie grumbled, shaking her head.

"It's not a huge secret, Marshal, but it's not exactly Frontier Ledger news either. Besides, I've been here longer than both of you, so I've seen a lot. And, people like to talk, especially to the preacher." He smiled. "Anyway, I'll see you at service tomorrow, Ellie?"

"Wouldn't miss it," she replied with a smile.

"Marshal?" he asked. "Care to grace us with your presence?"

Jessie shook her head. "I'm afraid not this time."

"I'll leave your stool out in case you change your mind."

She nodded.

*

Elmer poured a hot cup of coffee that had just been brewed on the small cook stove in the back, and slid it across the bar as the door swung open. Most of the patrons were gathered around the Dice and Faro games. A handful danced in the middle of the floor, and a few others were seated at tables with saloon girls in their laps. Three more sat on stools along the bar.

"This is probably the last of our quiet nights," he said.

"Yeah," Jessie agreed, picking up the mug and tossing back a long swallow of the burning liquid. She felt like having a glass of whiskey, but she didn't need to be teetering on the inebriation scale in case someone decided they didn't like the way the dice was rolled and wanted to start a fight. Luckily, they hadn't had much of that lately, but she and Bert still patrolled through town every night, making a special point to hang out in the saloon until the majority of the gamblers had left, or simply run out of money. They also spent a lot of time around Six Gun Alley, which was where most of the trouble happened.

"Want me to top that off for you?" Elmer asked as Jessie peered across the room, making eye contact with Bert, who was sitting at their usual table in the back corner.

"Nah, I'm good for now," she replied, walking away.

"It's getting cooler," Bert said as she sat down adjacent to him, facing the rest of the room.

Jessie nodded in agreement. The coldest and hottest months always brought trouble, mostly because everyone was cooped up inside to keep warm or cool down out of the sun. With the Rustler's Den being the only saloon in town, and essentially the only place for entertainment since the theatre had closed a year and a half earlier, it was the center of attention during the peak seasons.

"Do you rent or own your house?" she asked, seemingly out of the blue.

"What?"

"Your house...rent or own?"

"Oh, we own it...Well, the bank owns it and we make mortgage payments. Why? Are you and Ellie looking to buy a house? I hear the one at the edge of town is for sale."

Jessie sipped her coffee. "I'm not buying anything, although I think at some point Ellie would be happy if we settled into a house. Anyway, did you buy your house from the mayor?"

"Yes. The town owns all of the real estate. The mayor decides when and what properties to sell off. You didn't know this?"

"No."

"It's pretty much how Boone Creek became a town, and why it's still thriving today. The businesses you see around town are all owned by the people who run them, but they purchased the land or building from the town if they were the original owner."

"It certainly makes sense," Jessie said, waving at Elmer for another cup of coffee. "I just walked the streets, and it's quiet in here. Why don't you head home for the night. I'm sure Molly could use a break."

"Are you sure? Eddie has been giving her a fit lately, I'm pretty sure he has teeth coming in," he said, referring to their four-month old son, Edgar Bertholomew Boleyn.

"I'll be fine. I'm going to call it an early night myself."

Bert tied the scarf around his neck to help ward off the chill of the night air. "Looks like we'll have snow soon," he said, glancing at the sky when he opened the door. "Maybe the cold snow will help Eddie's sore gums."

"Yeah. Although, I'm not looking forward to the slushy streets."

"Me either," Bert replied with a wave as he left.

TWO

Ellie awoke before the sunrise and lit a walking candle to see her way around the large room above the General Trade, which she and Jessie called home. Pulling on her chemise and under skirt, she felt arms encircle her waist and a warm body pressed against her back. "I didn't mean to wake you," she whispered, turning to kiss Jessie tenderly.

"You didn't," Jessie replied, her arms still around Ellie's waist. "I had trouble sleeping."

"Do you want me to make you something to eat?"

"No," Jessie murmured, shaking her head as she pulled Ellie's chemise over her head, draping it over the dressing chair behind her. Their lips inched closer and closer until they were merely a breath apart.

Ellie watched the candlelight flicker in Jessie's bright green eyes as her heart fluttered faster and faster. Every time they made love, it was like the first time all over again. She couldn't get enough and never wanted it to end. She barely blinked as Jessie led her back towards the bed, careful not to close the miniscule distance between them just yet.

"You're the most beautiful woman I've ever laid eyes on," Jessie murmured, following as Ellie lied on her back. She moved over her, sliding their bodies together.

"Touch me," Ellie whispered.

Obliging, Jessie ran her hand up Ellie's thigh. The silky skin under her shivered as her hand crossed over Ellie's slender abdomen, easing its way further up. Her hand closed over a bare breast as their lips met in a heated kiss.

Ellie's lips quivered against Jessie's. She wrapped her arms around Jessie's shoulders and ran her hands up and down the smooth skin of her back. The flame of the candle danced along the wall, casting them in a delicate, orange glow.

Jessie pulled her mouth from Ellie's, gently caressing the tender skin of her neck and chest with her lips. Moving agonizingly slow, she dragged her tongue over a taut pink nipple, and slid her hand back down between Ellie's thighs. Warm wetness coated her fingers as she slipped them between the sensitive, swollen folds, begging for her touch. She matched the circular motion of her fingers to the urging rhythm of Ellie's hips as she suckled her breasts.

Ellie's legs spread further on their own accord. She gasped as Jessie's fingers pushed inside of her with a slow, steady thrusting that drove her quickly to the top of her peak. She held Jessie tightly as her body trembled.

Jessie moved to the side, pulling her wife into her arms.

"You make me feel like I've never felt before," Ellie murmured, still slightly breathless as she ran her hand up and down Jessie's torso, caressing her breasts and moving lower with each pass.

"Yeah," Jessie mumbled incoherently.

Ellie smiled before meeting her lips in a sensual kiss. After two years of making love with another woman, she was no longer tentative. She slid her fingers through the wetness awaiting her, similar to the way Jessie had touched her, swishing them in languid circles.

The kiss never broke between them as Ellie took Jessie's heightened senses over the edge. Her hips rose, encouraging Ellie to continue as another wave of pleasure washed over.

Breathing heavily, Jessie broke the kiss and reached down, pulling Ellie's hand away, then she slid it up between them. "I love you," she whispered, watching the flicker of the candle in her eyes.

"I love you, too," Ellie said, kissing her softly once more.

*

"Anything good in there?" Bert asked, glancing at Jessie who was sitting at her desk, with her boots propped up on the corner. She was reading the front page of the Frontier Ledger newspaper, which was delivered from Red Rock once a week.

"Two Wells Fargo stages were robbed outside of Dodge City last month."

"You think they'll head west?"

"If it were me...I would," she replied, folding the paper and placing it on the corner of her desk as she dropped her feet to the ground.

Bert peered through the open doorway and smiled, seeing his wife walking towards their building, pushing a baby buggy with mini horse-cart wheels under a thin frame and a wicker basket on top. "Well, hello," he said, cheerfully.

Curious, Jessie got up from her desk and followed him outside. Molly was lifting the little boy from the carriage, wrapping him in a thick blanket, as she walked over. "He's getting big," she said.

"I know. He does nothing but eat...all day long," Molly sighed. "Want to hold him?"

Jessie wasn't much on babies, but Ellie had helped Molly through her pregnancy and childbirth, subsequently becoming close friends with her. Therefore, they spent a lot of time with Bert, Molly, and baby Eddie. The more Jessie saw him, the easier handling him became. "Sure," she replied, holding her arms out.

"I told you she had a soft side," Ellie called with a laugh from the front door of her store, across the street, where she stood with her hands on her slim hips.

"What's that supposed to mean?" Jessie huffed, cradling the baby against her chest as he wiggled out of the top of his blanket. He ran his tiny fingers over her tie, then reached up for the brim of her hat. He was a spitting image of Bert, minus the mustache and goatee.

Molly giggled.

Jessie handed Bert his child, then proceeded the rest of the way across the street. "Care to elaborate on my soft side, Mrs. Henry?" Jessie questioned.

"I did…this morning as a matter of fact," Ellie teased as she stepped inside.

Jessie followed her in, removing her hat, and placing a soft kiss on her wife's lips.

"Isn't he just the cutest thing you've ever seen?" Ellie said, glancing back out at the street.

"He's certainly something," Jessie replied. "Does it bother you that we can't have children…together, I mean?"

Ellie shook her head. "No. I knew going into our marriage that wasn't a possibility. I'm pretty sure I can't have them anyway. At least, not after my first marriage." Ellie met Jessie's caring eyes and smiled. "You're enough for me. I'm happy, and I love you with all of my heart, Jessie."

"I love you, too," Jessie replied, kissing her again, just before Molly strolled inside with Eddie back in the buggy.

"I'll leave you ladies to it," she said with a wink as she stepped away, putting her hat back on as she went out the door.

*

Mayor Horace Montgomery was sitting at the desk in his office, which was on the second floor of the mayor's house, reading through the same newspaper that Jessie has perused earlier that morning.

"Cigar?" he asked, opening the box as Jessie sat down across from him.

Jessie nodded as she grabbed one of the neatly rolled cheroots and lit it. "I assume you know about the stage robberies in Dodge," she said, referring to the paper.

"I do."

"And?"

Mayor Montgomery ran his fingers over his thick, gray mustache. "Dodge City is quite a ways from here. I don't see the need to add extra deputies. Besides, Boone Creek is a much smaller town. I doubt those bandits will be looking to hit our bank stage." He folded his hands on the top of his desk and leaned back. "Jessie, you've done a damn good job as Town Marshal, and with only one deputy to boot."

"I've been shot, shot at, ambushed...shall I go on?" She shook her head. "The need for an extra deputy is apparent now more than ever. Bert and I can handle the nuisance of the town, but these gangs who are robbing banks and stages are much larger. We'd be greatly outnumbered if they decided to hit Boone Creek."

"I don't think one extra deputy will make that much difference," he replied.

Agreeing to disagree, Jessie thanked him for the cigar and left. "Stubborn old man," she spat as she stepped outside. The sun was shining brightly, but the air was significantly cooler than it had been just a few days earlier. Deciding to take a walk around town, she headed down Main Street Curve towards Center Street, which would take her to Six Gun Alley. It was quiet on the streets, but that was fairly normal for midday.

"Well, look at what the cat dragged in," Miss Mable drawled when she saw Jessie coming down the alley in front of the brothel.

"Afternoon," Jessie said.

"Still enjoying the married life?"

"Absolutely." Jessie smiled and waved as she kept walking.

*

Later that night, after a couple of casual walks around town, Jessie curled up in bed behind Ellie, draping an arm over her waist.

"Quiet night?" Ellie asked.

"Uh huh."

"I think I've gotten used to the ruckus. It's a bit unnerving how quiet the town has been lately," Ellie said.

"I like it quiet. That means no one is shooting at me," Jessie mumbled.

Ellie turned in her arms. "I don't want to think about people shooting at you."

"Good. Me either," Jessie replied, closing the short distance between their lips with a sensual kiss that left them both wanting more.

THREE

Jessie walked into the Marshal's office around her usual time, carrying the newspaper she'd just picked up, and a fresh cup of coffee.

"Go on! Get out of here!" Bert yelled as he stormed towards the door, and directly into her path, swinging a large stick.

Before Jessie could figure out what was going on, Bert crashed into her, sending the paper and her coffee mug flying through the air. The coffee splashed all over the front of her suit and drenched the newspaper on the way to the ground. The mug hit the wooden floor and smashed to pieces.

"Son of a bitch!" Jessie yelped.

Bert snatched the paper off the ground like a mad man, tossed it in the corner, and smashed the stick against it as hard as he could several times.

"I got it! I got it!" he yelled.

"Got what? Have you lost your damn mind?" she growled, trying to peel the hot, wet clothing from her skin.

"The mouse! I killed it!" he exclaimed, removing the paper and revealing the half beaten carcass of a small farm mouse.

"Are you serious? You ruined my paper and my suit, scalding me with hot coffee, because of a God damn mouse!" she yelled.

"I can't stand the things," he grimaced.

"Uh huh..." she trailed off, gritting her teeth and shaking her head as she turned to go back out the door.

While crossing the street, Jessie ignored the couple of town folk who'd said hello to her.

"Oh my! What happened to you?" Ellie asked when Jessie walked into the General Trade.

"Apparently, Bert is scared of mice."

"Mice? What?"

"He damn near knocked me out with a stick while he bashed a mouse to death. Your *good* mug didn't make it out alive. My suit didn't fare much better, I'm afraid, and neither did my newspaper for that matter. I'm so mad I could pistol whip him."

Ellie stood with her brows raised. "All of this over a mouse?"

"Yes."

"And he killed it?"

"I'm pretty sure it was headless by the time he'd finished."

"Aww, poor thing."

"Him or the mouse?"

"I guess both," Ellie laughed. "Come on, let's get you cleaned up. If I don't start soaking that white shirt now, I'll never get the coffee stain out of it. It's a good thing you like black. Otherwise, your entire suit would probably be ruined. You do smell delightful though." She grinned over her shoulder as she headed up the spiral staircase that led to their room.

"Are you sure you want to mess with it? I can take it down to Ike."

"I told you when we got married, I'm your wife. I can do your laundry with my own. There's no need to pay the tailor to tend to your clothing."

Jessie began removing her attire until she was left in her under clothes. "It's a good thing I have two suits," she muttered as she began redressing.

"I'll wash these out and get them on the line. Everything will be dry by morning, except the shirt. I'll soak it for a couple of days."

"Thank you." Jessie smiled, kissing her on the cheek.

"I honestly feel bad for Bert."

"Why is that?"

"He's a grown man who is scared of a mouse."

"It wasn't any bigger than this," Jessie said, holding her thumb and first finger about three inches apart. "Head to tail."

"Aww."

"I should go around and collect as many mice as I can and put them all in his desk."

"You finally gave him a desk?" Ellie questioned.

"I gave him some space and told him if he wanted a desk, he had to build one. I'm pretty sure he paid the stable hand at the livery to do it with some old scrap wood. Anyway, he now has his own work area, so he can leave mine alone."

"Well, that was nice of you. I'm surprised you didn't tell me...or Molly for that matter."

"Probably slipped my mind, and from what I hear, Eddie is a bit of a handful."

"Oh, yes he is. Molly's nipples are raw and have been bleeding from breastfeeding, and she said he's teething, so it's only going to get worse."

"I love you, and he's an adorable baby, but I don't need to know about Molly's nipples."

Ellie laughed.

15

"I'll see you for supper, unless I'm burying Bert's body because he swung that damn stick at me again."

"At least he wasn't trying to shoot the mouse!" Ellie called as Jessie headed back down the stairs.

Jessie chuckled, but honestly, Ellie was right. It could've been a lot worse.

*

"I'm—" Bert started, but Jessie cut him off.

"I don't want to hear it. I've moved on, but if you ever come at me, flailing a stick again, I'm going to shoot you. Are we clear?"

"Yes," he gulped. "For the record—"

"It was a mouse, Bert. A fucking little bitty mouse! I could see if it was a rattlesnake…but a mouse?!" She shook her head. He tried to talk again, but she held up her hand.

"Marshal?" a kid called from the doorway.

Jessie walked over and stepped out onto the sidewalk. "What can I do for you?"

"The mayor sent me to get you," he said.

She nodded and handed him a couple of bit coins from her vest pocket. "I better go see what he wants," she said to Bert as the kid ran off. "Watch out for that gang of giant mice."

"Funny," he mumbled.

*

The mayor was obviously waiting for her arrival since she saw him in front of the window, looking down at the street below.

"Mayor," she said, tipping her hat. "Everything okay?"

"Have you read the paper this morning?" he asked.

"No, not yet. Bert and I had a bit of a debacle. What's going on?"

He walked past her and grabbed the Frontier Ledger from his desk. "You smell like coffee."

"Part of the debacle. Don't ask," she sighed, reading over the front page.

The headline read: *Dodge City Bank Robbed By Four Gunmen Who Murder Two And Get Away!*

"I can't say I didn't see this coming, especially with all of the stage robberies," she said.

Mayor Montgomery chewed the edge of his mustache. "I'm going to have to work on the budget, so I can't make any promises. Make sure you and Bert are prepared in case they move west, and warn the bank."

"I'll wire the Marshal there and see if they have any idea who the gang is."

"Good call."

"Have you finished reading all of this?" she asked, still holding the paper.

"Yes."

"Do you mind if I take it? Mine was used for a massacre."

Mayor Montgomery gave her an odd look, but nodded.

"Thanks. I'll let you know what I find out. One quick question, what's going on with the Rayburn House?"

"It's still for sale. I haven't had a single offer. Why, are you interested?"

Jessie pondered in thought for a minute. She wasn't sure if Ellie was serious about wanting a house, but she'd been taking more walks with Jessie in the evenings, pausing to look at the little house each time.

"Here's the info sheet. Take a look and let me know what you think," the mayor said, handing her a piece of paper.

*

Jessie folded the house info and slid it into her coat pocket, then she perused the paper as she walked back towards the Marshal's Office. The second page continued with major national news, which was mostly about the railroad expansion, but horse-thieving had become quite popular, and seemed to be the most popularly reported crime. She stopped in the middle of the street, feeling her chest cave in as she read the names she hoped she'd never see. *William Doyle and Billy Doyle of the Eldorado Gang were captured in Castor Valley, Texas and are set to stand trial for the murder of Samuel Harvey.* "No," she whispered, shaking her head as she put her closed fist to her mouth to try and regain her composure.

"Everything okay?" Pastor Noah asked, watching her from the open doorway of the church.

"Yeah," she said, folding the paper under her arm. "You ever get a bit of bad news, Pastor, and you're not quite sure how to digest it?"

"Well...sure."

"What if you're responsible?"

"In that case, you probably need to do a little more than just digest it, don't you agree?"

Jessie nodded.

"My door is always open."

"I know," she replied as she tipped her hat and began walking again. Jessie couldn't say she hadn't thought of William and Billy over the past two years, but her life had changed so drastically since arriving in Boone Creek. Her time with the Eldorado Gang…as *La Diabla*, their fearless leader, seemed like a lifetime ago.

As Jessie rounded the corner, she spotted Otis meandering along, drunk as usual. He opened his mouth to speak, which was usually an insult directed at her.

"Not today, Otis. I'm liable to shoot you," she muttered, passing by.

"So, you're threatening me, now? Did anyone else here that? Lady Law says she's going to shoot me if I talk!" he yelled.

"Damn drunk!" Jessie growled as she kept walking.

Ellie was outside, updating the sales on her chalkboard, when she heard Otis shouting. She glanced up to see Jessie headed her way. "Hey, you," Ellie said with a smile. "What's Otis's problem today?"

"I'm not in the mood for his mouth, and I told him so. He didn't take it very well."

"Is everything okay? Don't tell me there's another mouse in the Marshal's Office."

"No. We're rodent free at the moment. I do have something to tell you though." Jessie stepped inside the store and took a look around to make sure they were alone.

"What's wrong?" Ellie questioned, following her.

Jessie handed her the paper and pointed to the column about the gang. She watched the changes in Ellie's face as she read it.

"This is your old gang, isn't it?"

Jessie nodded.

"I'm sorry."

"I have to go help them, Ellie. They're not murderers."

"Your life is here now," she said. "You were their leader. If you go, you'll be arrested, too."

"I know, but that's a chance I have to take. I'm sorry."

Tears slowly rolled down Ellie's soft cheeks. "Why?" she whispered. "Why are they more important than your wife and the life we've built together?"

Jessie moved closer. "Ellie…"

"Why are they more important than the town that stood behind you when the truth came out?"

"This isn't about Boone Creek…or about you."

"What is it then? Answer me!" Ellie growled.

"They are my brothers," Jessie muttered.

"What? Because you ran a gang together? That doesn't make people your family, Jessie. Love…that's what makes a family. You and I are a family."

"Ellie…" Jessie sighed. "They are my family, too. We share the same father." She grabbed her wife's hand and led her over to a pair of stools behind the counter. After a deep breath, which she let out slowly, and a long pause that seemed to last forever, Jessie lost herself in the story she'd never told another soul.

FOUR

"After the Mexican-American war ended in 1848, Texas became a state, and small towns started popping up all over as people spread south, into the lush farmlands. By 1850, a small town named Castor Valley had been established near San Antonio. With the immigrant boom, people began pouring into Texas, and Castor Valley soon became a popular place. Harlots like Gertie Henry, who was barely twenty years old, entertained the masses of men that paraded in and out of town. By 1854, Gertie had nearly a dozen regular gentlemen callers. One specific Irishman named Johnny Doyle, visited with her at least twice a week. He was a few years older than her and was often seen fighting over territory with the Germans in the street."

"How do you know all of this?" Ellie asked.

"Some of it Gertie told me, but I learned about the state history in school. Anyway, in 1855, Gertie found herself with child, Johnny Doyle's child to be exact. Having a pregnant whore in the brothel was bad for business, so she was forced to hide it until her belly revealed her secret. When she informed Johnny, he left and that was the last she saw of him."

"Oh, that's awful."

Jessie nodded and went on. "In the fall of that year, she gave birth to me. I was passed around from whore to whore during the day and throughout the night so they could keep me quiet. If any man heard a baby crying, he'd be out the door so fast, he'd barely have his clothes back on. The only reason Gertie wasn't kicked out of the brothel was because she was very popular and brought in a lot of men. Most of them referred to her as 'Good Gertie' on account she was good in bed."

Jessie checked the time on her watch before continuing. "Over the next fourteen years, I lived in the whorehouse, going to school with the rest of the kids from town during the day, and spent a lot of nights up on the roof, looking at the stars. I was about seven when we were walking through town, Gertie and I, having just left the general store. A horse and buggy was parked along the sidewalk with a woman and two small boys, a little younger than I was, sitting up top. Gertie spotted a man headed towards it and quickly snatched me along. 'Johnny,' she called out, and the man turned around. He pretended not to know her as she shoved me closer to him, claiming I was his. The woman in the buggy had a fit and the man shooed Gertie away, telling her she was crazy. I'm pretty sure the woman believed my mother because I looked more like the man than her two boys did. In any case, we never saw them again."

"So, that was your two brothers…in the buggy?"

"Yes."

"How did you find them?"

"That's an even longer story. I should probably get back to Bert before something else scares him," Jessie said.

"Oh, he's a grown man. I'm sure he can manage. Keep going," Ellie urged.

"Are you sure you want to hear all of this?"

"Of course. I've tried to get you to talk about your past several times."

"I don't talk about it because I left it behind when I moved on with my life. Same as you."

Ellie gave her a stern look.

"All right," she sighed. "We never went to church because we weren't welcomed, so the stars I studied every night never symbolized heaven to me. I didn't even know what heaven was until years later. Anyhow, the brothel wasn't the best place to grow up, but it was my home…the only home I ever knew until I met you," she said, squeezing Ellie's hand. "Although, I was teased for being a whore's daughter, it was the Irish blood running through my veins that gave me a temper like a rattlesnake. I won more than my fair share of fights as a kid. Gertie would always tell me 'Stop all this fighting. No man is going to want you if you're covered in scars.' It didn't bother me because I didn't want a man anyway."

Ellie giggled.

"What?" Jessie questioned.

"Nothing." Ellie grinned.

"Just after my fifteenth birthday, Gertie told me she had a big surprise, which was unusual. My birthdays were usually spent on the rooftop with something I'd stolen from a store. We didn't have any money, and Gertie certainly never gave me any of her 'earnings'. I worked with the horses at the stable and cattle in the corral to pay for material for one of the ladies to sew me new clothes each time I got bigger. However, on this birthday, she presented me with a dress, much like the ones she and the other ladies wore, and a key to one of the rooms."

"Oh my God, she tried to turn you out? At fifteen? Her little girl?" Ellie grimaced in shock.

Jessie nodded. "After two years of me refusing to be a whore, which caused some nasty arguments, I packed the few things I owned and rode over to San Antonio, which was a little more than a day's ride, on a stolen horse. There, I met a man named Joe Clarence. He was older, mid forties, and had fought for the south in the war. He was in town looking for someone to help with his cattle business. He didn't move large herds, but he did travel them a long distance across the border from Mexico to Texas, so one helper was all he was looking for. Since I was good on a horse and had worked cattle before, we made a deal. I had no home and no family, so going out on the trail with him seemed like a good idea. Truth be told, it was…for about two years. Joe was like the father I never had. He taught me how to skin an animal, shoot a straight shot with my eyes closed, play dice, drink whiskey, and even smoke a cigar properly. When we weren't driving cattle, he was teaching me everything he would've taught his son, had he had one. I even made a little money for myself."

Ellie noticed a change in Jessie as her shoulders stiffened.

"Everything changed one night. We were sitting by the campfire, passing a bottle of whiskey back and forth, and looking at the stars. That's when Joe tried to kiss me. He'd never acted as if he were sweet on me or interested in something other than our friendship, until that moment. I refused and backed away from him, blaming the poison we were drinking, but he grew angry. Before I knew it, he lurched at me. I fell back and he climbed on top of me. I'd seen him get mad a time or two, but I'd never seen the rage that was in his eyes that night as he held me down. I tried to talk to him, but he began fumbling with my clothing, trying to get my trousers open as he growled, 'It's about time you give me what's owed to me, you whore. I took you in, gave you work, fed you food, and what have you given me? Nothing!' I was in shock. Here was this man who was like a father to me, and he was attacking me. I yelled for him to get off of me, but he kept going, snatching at my clothing until the buttons popped open. By that time, I'd realized what his intention was. I fought back as hard as I could until I finally grabbed a hold of his manhood, which was hanging out of his open trousers. Luckily, he hadn't gotten my clothing completely open. I squeezed as hard as I could, digging my fingernails in until I removed skin, causing him to bleed and scream like a wild animal. He jerked back, smacking me across the face before crumbling to my side, writhing in pain. 'You bitch! You'll die for this!' he yelled, reaching for his pistol." She stopped for a second, staring at the floor as the memory flooded back to her.

"I'm sorry," Ellie whispered.

"It's okay, just been a long a time," Jessie said, before moving on. "Scared for my life, I grabbed my own pistol, the one he'd given me when he taught me how to shoot it. He was still wincing in pain as he fired a shot, which narrowly missed me as it hit his horse a few feet away. Before the horse fell to the ground, I aimed and fired my gun, putting a hole right in the middle of his forehead."

Ellie gasped as her free hand went to her mouth.

"I sat there for what felt like hours, staring at his dead body as the flames of the fire cast dancing shadows over him. I cried; I screamed; I even kicked him several times. The only thing that had ever felt like a real family, had betrayed me, too. Knowing I needed to be as far away from that spot as I could when day broke, I went through his pack, taking all of his money and anything that was valuable, and I set out on my horse."

Listening to Jessie tell her story, made Ellie understand the woman she'd given her heart to, all the more. Jessie was a puzzle that no one had ever figured out, not even Ellie, but she'd put together enough pieces to find the remarkable, caring, and loving woman buried deep inside. Hearing the story only added more of the missing pieces, and slowly the woman beside her, whom she'd given her love and life to, was becoming whole. Ellie's heart broke for her. "You're amazing, you know that?" she said, leaning in and kissing Jessie's cheek.

"How so?" Jessie questioned.

"I've never met anyone like you, and probably never will again."

"Does that mean you've heard enough of my dismal story?" Jessie said. She had been cautious at first. Telling Ellie everything, meant telling her a lot of bad things…things Jessie wasn't proud of. The last thing she wanted was for her wife to look down on her, but the golden slivers in Ellie's brown eyes sparkled as her lips formed a beautiful smile that tugged at Jessie's heart. One thing they'd both learned in the past two years, was their love really was unconditional.

"Of course not," Ellie murmured. "And it's not dismal. It's your life. I want to know all of it."

Jessie took a deep breath and continued. "I tried to get a job moving cattle with larger outfits, but no one wanted to hire a woman. I had saved a little money and with what I'd taken from Joe, I was able to bum around from town to town for a little over a year. I made a little money here and there playing dice. I was never any good at Faro.

"By this point, I was twenty and had no idea what I was going to do. I was down to my last bit coin, sitting in a saloon in a cow town between San Antonio and Castor Valley, drinking my troubles away. I hadn't paid much attention to the two young men who had sat down beside me, doing much of the same, until they made mention of their mother's recent passing from the fever. Neither of them looked old enough to be drinking, so I asked about their father. The older one shook his head and said 'Johnny Doyle ran off ten years ago to find gold in California, promising to return for all of us. We never heard from that son of a bitch again.' I set my drink down as they introduced themselves as William Doyle and Billy Doyle. The memory of meeting Johnny Doyle on the street when I was seven years old, came flooding back to me. I knew that they were my brothers, especially after they described their mother. She sounded identical to the woman who had been in the buggy with the two young boys. I neglected to tell them who I was, mostly because I had nothing to offer them anyway."

"It's amazing you even found them."

"Yeah, but as it turned out, they lived in the next town over, about from here to Pinewood, so they'd hadn't grown up that far away. Anyway, after I drank away the last of my money, I bid them farewell, but the boys followed me out of the saloon and down the street, wanting to know where I was headed as I walked towards my horse. I tried to scare them away, so I was honest. I said, 'I have nothing left, so I'm going to rob the next stage when it leaves town, take whatever I can get, and start a new life somewhere.' They had nothing left either, and when they asked to join me, I felt like I had an obligation to protect them. They were eighteen and sixteen, but to me, they were those little boys I remembered from my childhood." Jessie paused and shook her head. "I planned to rob the one stage, split the money with them, and send them on their way to start a life of their own, but one stage turned quickly into two, then three and four. It was too late to push them away at that point, so I formed the Eldorado Gang after the town where we met. They were okay shots, but I taught them how to shoot with their eyes closed, much in the same way Joe had taught me, and led them on a rampage of thievery all over Mexico, anonymous bounty hunting for other outlaw gangs in south Texas where we were virtually unknown, and crooked gambling in saloons and back alleys. We were feared by anyone crossing the Mexico/Texas border for about five years. We never intentionally killed anyone, we were thieves, but if we were shot at, we returned fire with nearly perfect accuracy.

"After we had enough money to settle down and get out of that life, which was my plan from the beginning, the boys wouldn't hear of it. I'd turned them into outlaws, and it tore me apart. I didn't want any more people to get hurt so that we could add a little more money to our pockets. There were huge bounties on our heads in both Texas and Mexico, probably still are. Anyhow, we didn't have a home because we were always on the run, and looking for our next hit. So, we pretty much set up camp in the middle of nowhere every night, mostly in Mexico. When the weather was bad, we went into towns where we were unknown, and bordered rooms at brothels. At one point, I couldn't do it anymore. I asked them one last time to pack up with me and leave Texas together, giving up the outlaw life, but they both refused. After they fell asleep that night, I went into our money bag and pulled out a little more than a quarter of what was in there, packed my pockets full of my necessities, and headed out on my horse. I rode all night long and all of the next day, until I was far enough away that they'd never find me. I slept against a rock, ate the little bit of tack and berries that I'd taken with me, and headed out once again. I eventually wound up back over the border in San Antonio. I knew I couldn't hang around there long, so I hopped on the first train headed west. I'd heard about Tombstone, but I was looking for something further away.

A place I knew the boys would never find me, so I went north from there. I hated leaving them behind, it literally broke my heart, but I knew seeing them again would only draw me right back to that life. I wanted something new. I wanted an actual life for myself. I don't condone what I did. I was wrong. We all were. We did what we had to do to get by. It's not an excuse, it just is what it is. I'm not proud of the Eldorado Gang, and *La Diabla* was a part of me that I left behind when I walked away from the gang...and my brothers."

"All of that time and you never told them you were their sister?"

"No," Jessie mumbled. "I was ashamed because I got them into a life of crime, when I should've protected them and gave them a proper home."

"How could you do that, when you yourself didn't have a proper home or upbringing?" Ellie questioned.

"They did. They were raised right. From the stories they told, they had an amazing mother. When she died, everything fell apart for them. Their house was rented, so when they couldn't pay, they were kicked out. They'd spent nearly all of their money to give their mother a deserving funeral. So, when they met me, they too were on their last couple of bits."

"It was fate that you happened to be in the same place that day."

"Fate or misfortune?"

"Jessie, how can you even ask that? They are your flesh and blood."

"I know. They were my responsibility, which is why I have to go help them. I got them into that mess. It's my fault. I can't let them hang, and if I don't go, they will."

"How do you know it's not a ploy to get you? You said it yourself, there are probably still warrants."

"I'll be careful. I used to have long hair, close to the length of yours. I cut it all off right before I got here and Muddy Joe finished the job."

"Really?" Ellie looked at her oddly.

"Yes. What's wrong?"

"I'm trying to picture you with long hair."

"Don't bother. I prefer it like this."

"I didn't say I didn't like your short hair." Ellie grinned. "When are you leaving?" she asked, getting back to the seriousness of the situation.

"First light so I can catch the train from Red Rock."

"I wish you weren't going."

"I know. I wish I didn't have to, but I know my brothers. They're not murderers."

"I'm scared, Jessie."

"I'll be okay. I promise," she replied, pulling Ellie into her arms and holding her tightly. "I've told you before, you're not going to lose me."

FIVE

Jessie watched the stars fade as faint shades of orange began to paint the sky, one stroke at a time. Gray clouds in the distance indicated the first real threat of snow. She slapped the reins, urging her horse to gallop a little faster down the wagon trail. The ride to Red Rock from Boone Creek was two days, and she was already on her second day, hoping to make the last train out that evening.

As she crossed the terrain, she thought back to the last time she'd taken that same ride. She and Bert were escorting a prisoner for his trial a year and a half earlier, and were ambushed right outside of Boone Creek. They were lucky to have escaped with their lives. The only other time she'd been on that trail was when she left her brothers and went out on her own, searching for a new life…the life she subsequently found in Boone Creek. Leaving her brothers had been the hardest thing she'd ever done…at that point. Now, she found it twice as hard leaving Ellie behind. She never thought she'd settle down, much less get married. Becoming a Town Marshal had started out as a huge burden; a penance she'd gladly put on herself as payback for all of her outlaw activity. In the two years that she'd been working on the other side of the law, with a metal badge pinned to her vest, she'd grown to like it.

Missing her new life already, she wondered if she'd made a bad decision to go help her brothers. She looked up at the sky once more, seeing an eagle soar overhead, seemingly going in the same direction to get away from the cold.

"I hope you're a sign," she whispered.

*

As morning turned into afternoon, and eventually night, Jessie rode on. Her butt and hips hurt from being in the saddle for so long. It had been a while since she'd ridden a horse for two days. She was tired and hungry, but she kept going until she saw the flicker of lights far off in the distance.

"Finally," she said, kicking the worn out horse into another gear. "We're almost there," she urged, petting the side of the animal's neck. He dashed along the trail as the city grew closer and closer.

Jessie wasn't looking forward to another couple of days traveling, but at least most of the rest would be by train. Plus, she could get a decent meal and eventually sleep in a hotel bed, instead of the ground.

*

The livery and stable was the first place Jessie went. Making sure her horse was boarded until she returned, she paid for four weeks in advance and told the kid to take good care of him if she never came back. He looked at her oddly, but nodded in agreement.

The train station was on the other side of town and the distinct sound of the locomotive whistle was already echoing through the streets. She picked up her pace from a brisk walk to a jog as she dodged people and wagons.

Finally making it to the station, she rushed up to the window, straightening her clothing at the same time. "One ticket on the Santa Fe Rail Line south to El Paso," she said. "Sleeping coach, if you have it."

"You're in luck. This one's leaving in five minutes," the man on the other side of the window replied. "It'll be fifteen dollars."

"Fifteen dollars!" she squeaked.

"First Class is all that's left. A lot of folks are headed down to Tombstone," he said.

The train whistle blew again, indicating two minutes. Jessie shook her head in disbelief, and handed the man one eagle and a half eagle coins. "Is it a sleeper?" she asked, taking the ticket.

"Sorry, those are all full."

Jessie grumbled as she rushed over to the platform. White clouds of steam bellowed out of the smokestack on top of the large locomotive. She checked her ticket and began searching for coach #6.

*

The first class coach had velvet lined, plush seating, and a storage compartment above her head for luggage. Since she'd ridden on horseback for two days to get to the train, she hadn't carried any regular luggage. Instead, she traveled with a knapsack made of cowhide, which held the necessary items she couldn't live without, plus, a shirt, a set of under clothes, a pair socks, and a pair of trousers. After tossing the knapsack into the compartment, she made sure her coin purse was tucked down in her vest pocket, before taking her seat as the train lurched forward.

Jessie waited for the train to get up to full speed underway before heading to the first class dining coach in search of something to entertain her empty, groveling stomach.

"Whiskey and a sandwich," she said to the man behind the bar.

He nodded and flipped a thimble cup over, pouring whiskey neatly to the top of it, careful not to spill a drop. Then, he reached into a lower compartment, pulling a paper-wrapped, corned beef sandwich. "That'll be one dollar," he said, sliding the food and drink across to her.

First class travel is definitely far more expensive than third class, she thought as she handed him a trade dollar coin. The last time she'd taken this same route, it had cost her five dollars, and there was no access to the dining coach. She'd had to take her chances with the food at the rail stops.

"You headed to Tombstone?" asked a gentleman in a fancy suit as he walked up next to her, also ordering a whiskey.

"No," she replied huskily, avoiding eye contact and disguising her voice. The least amount of people who knew who she was, or that she was a woman for that matter…the better. Ignoring him, she went back to her sandwich.

"My brother has been there for about a year. He and I are planning to open a gambling saloon," he continued.

Jessie didn't say anything as she finished her drink and slid the cup over, nodding in the barkeeps direction. She looked around at the people squeezed together at the small tables and was happy she'd chosen to sit at the bar.

"You ever been there? Tombstone, I mean?"

She turned back to the man next to her, shaking her head no before eating the last bite of her food as the barkeep slid over her drink. She gave him a trade dollar and held her hand up for him to keep the change. "If you'll excuse me," she said to the man next to her as she swallowed the burning liquor in one long sip, set down the cup, and walked through the door into the next coach.

*

Jessie pulled a match from her vest pocket, striking it against the sole of her boot. The orange flame flared up and she held it against her pocket watch. It was close to four a.m. and the train was scheduled to arrive in El Paso at 6:05a.m. She extinguished the match and sat up straighter, watching the stars in the sky as the darkness rushed by outside. Even though the sun hadn't begun to rise yet, she was sure she could see the Rio Grande.

After returning to her coach earlier that evening, she'd curled up as best she could against the wall in her wide seat, and had gotten about three and half hours of rest once the gentle rocking of the train coach, and dull sound of the wheels on the tracks, finally lulled her to sleep.

Jessie grinned, knowing she'd been correct about the location, when the locomotive began to slow. It eventually came to a grumbling halt in Albuquerque, New Mexico Territory, the final stop before El Paso, Texas. She stayed aboard, choosing to have a breakfast and coffee in the dining coach. The biscuit she'd eaten was nothing like Ellie's, and she'd thrown most of it away. However, the coffee wasn't half bad. She settled on two cups, then made her way back to her seat for the rest of her duration. Eating the biscuit had made her think of Ellie...and home, something she never thought she'd be able to say. It felt good knowing she had a home to come back to, and a loving, caring wife waiting for her. She'd hated putting Ellie and their life together behind the lives of her brothers, but she felt strongly that they wouldn't have been in that predicament in the first place if she hadn't turned them into outlaws. She only hoped they'd changed their ways after she'd left and this was a simple mishap they were caught up in, and nothing more. *If they really did murder this man…if they're still robbing and thieving, I'll be back on the next train out of there,* she mentally reminded herself.

*

The Santa Fe Rail Line came to a stop in El Paso. From there, Jessie purchased another pricy first class ticket aboard the South Pacific Rail Line, heading towards San Antonio, which was another ten-hour ride. She tried to pass the time by watching the scenery go by, but she'd seen enough Texas land to last a lifetime when she'd worked with Joe as a herder. That had been such a bittersweet time in her life. She wondered if it would've ended the same way if she could go back and do it all over again. The more she thought about it, the more she realized it would have. Whether or not Joe had drank that night, or if he was even drunk, didn't matter. His attitude had already begun shifting. She'd noticed the aggression, but he was like a father and she enjoyed working with him, so she'd let it go. The night he'd attacked her was almost like everything that had been building up had finally boiled over, and his true self appeared like a wolf in sheep's clothing. Thinking about that dreadful time in her life only angered her.

Taking a deep breath, she let it out slowly. "You can't change your past, and you can't change who you are," she whispered.

As she fought off the urge to sleep, untrustworthy of the people around her, especially in the daylight when she'd surely be the only person resting, she focused her mind on her brothers and what they were probably going through at that moment. She'd never been jailed, but she'd certainly locked up enough people since becoming a Town Marshal. None of them ever seemed to take it well.

*

Morning slowly turned into afternoon as the train made its appointed rail stops. Jessie had opted for a bowl of beef broth soup and another sandwich in the dining coach, when her stomach began rumbling loud enough for those around her to notice.

After the final stop, the locomotive chugged on, hitting speeds of close to sixty-five miles per hour in some areas along the flat, dessert-like terrain, before pulling into the San Antonio station just after five p.m.

Jessie grabbed her knapsack and disembarked with a couple dozen people who scattered about, heading further into the city. She turned down a side alley and came to a stop, removing two small glass jars from her satchel. One contained short clippings of her hair from the last time Muddy Joe had cut it. The other was a glue-like substance made from salve, bees wax, and milk casein. Jessie shook the bottle of liquid, mixing it thoroughly. Then, she spread some of it across her upper lip with her finger and waited. It smelled horribly, but it stuck to her face and felt almost rubbery. She peeled it from one side, and it came off her skin in a perfect strip. She sighed in relief that it had actually worked. Then, she stuck her finger back in the liquid, this time spreading it over the rubbery flap, before swiping it through the jar of hair. The freshly cut, blonde hair bonded to the flap and quickly dried in the air. She examined it on both sides, making sure everything held together, then she wiped a thick layer of the liquid glue onto her upper lip once more and carefully affixed the flap to it, creating the perfect fake mustache. She let it dry for a couple of minutes, then checked the glue to make sure it was holding. As she tugged on the hairs, it also pulled the skin of her upper lip. "I hope I can get this off, or Ellie's not going to be happy with me," she muttered, closing everything up and tucking it neatly into her knapsack.

She walked towards the stable and livery to see about a horse, but stopped when she passed by the stage office. She could possibly cut the half a day's ride time down by taking a stage, versus going alone on horseback. Plus, her chances of being noticed or even approached by someone who knew her, was much slimmer.

"May I help you, sir?" the stage driver asked.

"How much to take me to Castor Valley?" she questioned, happy that the newly added facial hair was working as a disguise. The last thing she needed was someone to figure out who she was.

"Round trip?" he asked.

"One way."

"It's five dollars for a full stage."

"It'll just be me," she replied, handing him a half eagle coin.

"Let me close up the office and we'll be on our way."

"Wonderful. Do you mind if I wait inside?"

"No. Go right ahead, sir," he said, holding the door open.

Jessie climbed up inside and sat down on the plush velvet seat. She'd never ridden in a stagecoach before, but she'd robbed enough of them to know that some were very luxurious, and much more comfortable than riding in a saddle for a long period of time.

*

True to his word, the stage driver had returned quickly, and they set out on the journey to the next town over. He'd tried to make small talk with Jessie, but she simply told him she was a lawyer, heading there for a trial. When he began asking questions, she told him she'd just gotten off a long train ride and excused herself from conversation so that she could get some sleep.

He obliged and drove on as she did her best to get comfortable as the carriage rattled along, bouncing down the trail. With only one passenger, there wasn't much weight to hold it down, so the faster the driver directed the horses, the more it recoiled. Jessie found it nearly impossible to sleep at first, but eventually she dozed off.

SIX

Castor Valley, State of Texas

Early November 1882

"Whoa!" the driver yelled.

Jessie stiffened, reaching for the pistol she had tucked in the back of her trousers in case she were to run into trouble along the journey. Being the Town Marshal of Boone Creek had no merit once she left the town limit, and especially outside of Colorado Territory. She slowly sat up, unsure of what was going on. That's when she saw the lights and noticed the sound of a bustling town. It was almost midnight and people were milling about, walking down the sidewalks and in the street. The sound of a piano could be heard when the doors of the nearby saloon opened.

She felt like she'd just fallen down a hole and been taken back in time. Her stomach was in knots. She never thought she'd step foot in Texas ever again, much less Castor Valley.

"Here we are," the driver said, opening the door. "The Grand Hotel is on Dodd Row, which is the next street over. We're on Central Street here. If you cut across Third Street right up there, you'll see the hotel."

"Thanks," she replied, exiting with her knapsack thrown over her shoulder.

The driver had pointed the way, but Jessie hadn't needed his direction. Not much had changed in the years that she'd been gone. It even had the same rancid smell, which had always reminded her of dirty bathing water.

She hitched her pack up a little higher on her shoulder, pulled the brim of her hat a little lower, and tucked her chin as she walked away. Choosing not to pass in front of the brothel that was once her home, she headed in the other direction, cutting across Second Street, which was on the other side of the Cattleman's Saloon, and ran between it and the Valley Opera House. She glanced to her right, across Central Street, towards the general store and bank. Myer Alley, the street behind them, was where several buildings were located, including the Sheriff's Office and jail. Thinking about William and Billy, knowing that was where they were, made her sigh audibly.

Two drunkards barreled out the front door of the saloon, narrowly missing her, and falling over each other as they struggled to fist fight. She hurried around the corner and out of harm's way in case they began shooting at one another. The last thing she needed was to be involved in an altercation, even as a witness. She'd been lying down when the stage entered town, so she wasn't sure if any law signs regarding firearms, were posted. All cities, and most towns, had done away with open carry, forcing people to check their guns with the sheriff's office upon entering the town limit.

Once she made it to Dodd Row, which ran parallel to Central Street and directly behind the saloon, she turned left, passing the stable and livery where she'd spent most of her days, working with the animals. She noticed they'd added a wagon repair shop on one end. If there was one place in Castor Valley that had felt like home, it was that building. She smiled briefly, recalling the very first time she'd ever ridden a horse. It had been down that very same street. She'd nearly fallen off when the gelding sensed her nervousness and bucked, but she'd held on tightly to the reins and leaned forward, talking softly to the large animal. They calmed down together, then trotted down the middle of Dodd Row like they'd owned the town.

Shaking away the memory, Jessie pulled open the door of the hotel. In all of the years she'd lived in Castor Valley, she'd never been inside. A kerosene-fueled chandelier hung from the ceiling, and a fur rug was stretched across the floor in front of the wooden counter. A parlor was on the opposite side of the room, with velvet covered chairs and walnut tables in front of a fireplace. Another chandelier provided the sitting area with dim lighting.

"Good evening, sir. May I help you?" The man behind the counter yawned as he stood up from a chair.

"I'd like a room, please," Jessie requested.

"How many nights will you be staying with us?" he asked, flipping the page in the log book.

"I'm not certain. I'm in town on business and may be here for a few days."

The man nodded and ran his finger down the page. "Here we are. Room 204 is available for at least a week. It's one dollar per day. All meals are included, as is one bath every five days."

"I hope to be on my way home within the week," she mumbled, handing him a half eagle coin to cover her stay for the next five days.

"What is your name?" he asked, dipping the quill in ink.

Jessie hadn't thought about a fake name to go with her disguise. She quickly thought of that first horse she'd ridden. "Homer," she answered, using the gelding's name. "J. D. Homer, Esquire," she added, giving the full name and title. She'd used J for Jessie and D for Diabla, the only two names she'd ever been known by, which would be easy to remember. And since she was pretending to be the boys' lawyer, which was the only way she'd be able to see them, she made sure her title was known, in case people starting asking around about her.

He wrote the name in the book next to the room number, and handed her a skeleton key. "Here you are, Mr. Homer. Take the stairs to the upper level. The room will be down on the right," he said.

She nodded and made her way up to her accommodation.

The room was over-sized with a double bed, dresser, and nightstand, as well as a small desk with a chair. Another table sat on the opposite side of the room with a wash basin on top of it and a chamber pot underneath.

Jessie locked the door and peeled off her mustache, which took a little effort and nearly caused her to shriek in pain. "Son of a bitch," she muttered, rubbing the tender skin above her upper lip. She decided to just leave it on next time, as she began removing her clothing in preparation for a much needed sleep.

*

The next morning, Jessie rose ahead of the sun and began dressing in her black suit. She looked through the window and down at the quiet street, as she put on her tie and fastened the buttons of her vest. It wouldn't be long before the hustle and bustle of the day began. After apply a thick layer of smelly glue above her lip, she stuck the fake mustache on, checking it in the mirror one last time, before heading down to a breakfast of eggs, sausage, and coffee.

A few gentlemen nodded in her direction and one lady smiled shyly at her, but Jessie generally kept to herself as she ate her meal. She hadn't traveled over one-thousand miles to make acquaintances. She was back in Castor Valley for one reason and that was to free her brothers.

As soon as she finished, Jessie put her hat on, tugging it down low as she walked out of the hotel. Still wanting to avoid the brothel, she turned left and followed the same path as the night before, down Dodd Row to Second Street, then Central Street, which was the main road running through the middle of town. She took the wide walkway between the bank/post building and the general store, which led her straight to Myer Alley in front of the Hen House Diner, the only building in the middle of the alley. The rest of the structures lined the street as it stretched parallel with Central street and Dodd Row. The sheriff's office and jail were to left, at the very end, giving them a good view of the folks coming and going from that end of town.

Jessie wasn't nervous, that never seemed to happen to her, but her senses were accelerated, making her alert to her surroundings. The morning air was thick and dry, and nowhere near as cool as it had been in Boone Creek when she'd left. She felt a bead of sweat on the side of her forehead, and quickly wiped it away as she made her way over to the sheriff's office.

"Good morning," the sheriff's deputy said, greeting her when she walked inside.

"Morning," she replied, tipping her hat. "I'm here to see my clients, William and Billy Doyle."

He looked oddly at her. "And you are?"

"I'm sorry," she apologized for not introducing herself. "I'm J. D. Homer, their hired attorney."

"I didn't know they had a lawyer."

"I was up in north Texas when I got word. It's taken me this long to get down here. I assume my clients are being handled properly."

"Well, yeah. They're in with all of the other prisoners who are awaiting trial."

"What exactly are they being charged with? My telegram wasn't very clear."

"Murder."

Jessie raised a brow. "That's all? No details?"

"The sheriff will have to give you all of that. He's not in yet."

"When he gets in, please inform him that I'd like to view the report and any witness statements. If I'm not here, I'm staying at the Grand Hotel."

"Yes, sir."

Jessie waited as her patience began to wear thin. "My clients?" she finally questioned.

"Oh, right. You want to see them," he said, waving for her to follow as he headed down a hallway.

The jail in the sheriff's office was nearly twice the size of the jail back in Boone Creek, and had six cells with iron bars, three on each side of the hall. Just as the jail back home, it wreaked of urine and the body odor of those desperately in need of a bath. She was glad she could still smell the faint stench of the mustache glue. As bad as it was, it paled in comparison to the jail.

"William and Billy Doyle, your lawyer is here," the deputy announced, unlocking the bars.

Jessie thought she'd know her brothers without a doubt, but she couldn't tell with their dingy clothing and full facial hair. All of the men seemed to blend together, until two of them stood up.

"We don't have an attorney," the slightly taller one said.

William! she thought, recognizing his voice. Her heart sank a little at the sight of them. Both of the men had scraggly beards and were dressed in frontier shirts, one a dull-red color, the other tan with faint stripes, along with brown frontier trousers and suspenders. Neither looked as if they'd had a bath, nor washed their clothing in over a month.

"This man says he's your lawyer, and he needs to talk to you, so come on!" the deputy snapped.

Both of the men stepped out of the cell, eyeing Jessie up and down, before following the deputy further down the hall to one of the empty cells on the opposite side of the hallway.

"I have to lock you in," he said to Jessie.

"I'll be fine," she answered.

"Who are you?" William asked.

"J. D. Homer, your attorney."

"We didn't hire any lawyer," Billy added.

"Someone must've done it for you," she replied, talking loud enough for the deputy to hear as he walked away, presumably back to his desk, but she wasn't sure. She waved the two young men in closer to her, then whispered, "*La Diabla*," in their ears.

William and Billy jerked back.

Jessie took off her hat and put her finger over the mustache. She watched as they both stared at her, shaking their heads in disbelief, then stared some more. She nodded and smiled as their eyes began to grow large. She moved her finger from the mustache to her lips.

"I'm waiting on the report from the sheriff, but I need you to tell me what happened," she said loudly.

"We were in the Cattleman's Saloon, minding our business and playing dice—"

Jessie cut him off. "Let's start with what you were doing in town."

"We moved after..." he paused, glancing at the hallway. "After leaving Mexico a year ago."

"Okay, back to the saloon," she redirected him.

"We weren't bothering with anyone," Billy said. "That crazy man was drunker than a loon. He pulled a pistol, shooting everything in sight, but us. William and I shot back before he killed one of us or someone else."

"Let me get this straight. He was shooting at you two first?"

"Yes," William stated. "He fired at least three, maybe four shots before Billy and I drew on him. I yelled for him to put the gun down."

"What did he do?"

"He aimed right at us!" Billy exclaimed.

"We both shot him as he was aiming to shoot again. He fell back as his bullet went up over our heads," William said.

"We weren't trying to kill him, honest. We shot him in the leg and shoulder, but he couldn't be saved. There was too much blood."

"When were you arrested by the sheriff's office?"

"Not long after. We told the truth, but he arrested us for disorderly conduct or something like that. When we got back here, the sheriff asked for our names, and we gave them. That's when he said, 'I know exactly who you are, and I know you murdered this man. You're both going to hang!'"

Jessie shook her head. This was worse than she'd thought. "Let's wait until I see the report from the sheriff, and we'll go from there. I'm going to do some digging around. I'll be back to see you in a day or so."

The young men nodded and shook her hand, knowing that it might give her away if they hugged her.

William pointed at her and mouthed the word: bounty. Then he held up five fingers, followed by a zero sign, twice.

Jessie looked oddly at him.

Shaking his head, William mouthed: Bounty on your head, $500.

Jessie nodded, finally understanding what he was saying. "Deputy!" she called.

He appeared quickly, which meant he was close by and not out front at the desk.

"I'm finished here…for now. Please have the sheriff send for me when he comes in. I'd like to read the arrest report and charges as soon as possible."

"Yes, sir," he replied.

Jessie hated leaving her brothers, but she had a lot of work ahead of her, and not a whole lot of idea how to do it. The thought of walking around town with a bounty on her head wasn't as exciting as it used to be, and only added to her discomfort of being back in Castor Valley to begin with.

On her way back towards the hotel, Jessie passed by the bank, which also housed the post. She needed to send word to Ellie that she'd arrived, so she walked inside.

"I need to send a telegram," she said.

"Where is it going?" the man behind the desk asked, holding a quill above an ink bottle, which sat next to a piece of paper.

"Boone Creek, Colorado Territory, addressed to Ellie Fray."

He wrote the information and waited for her to continue.

"Arrived. $500 prize. Post soon. Love," she said, giving him the cryptic message, before placing a trade dollar and a quarter on the counter to cover her post fee. She watched as he put the money in the register, then walked over to the wire machine to send it through. As soon as he finished, he wadded up the paper and threw it in the trash bin where it blended in with several others.

Hoping it had gone through, she tipped her hat and left. She noticed the saloon across the street when she stepped outside and knew that was where she needed to begin her search for the truth.

SEVEN

Jessie was surprised to see the couple of dozen people gathered around the gambling tables, and half a dozen more occupying stools at the bar in the mid-morning hours. The saloon back in Boone Creek was usually empty at that time of day. She slid onto a stool at the end and raised her hand up slightly to get the attention of the barkeep, who nodded in her direction, then filled the drink orders that he was currently working on. He was wearing a white, high-collared shirt with red garters on his upper arms, holding back his puffy sleeves, a black vest, and a red, ribbon tie, which was the typical dress for a saloon keeper. His head was bald in the middle, with thick hair on both sides that connected to the thick mutton chops covering his cheeks.

"What can I get for you?" the barkeep asked, finally making his way to Jessie's end of the bar.

"Whiskey," she answered.

He walked away and returned with a full thimble cup.

"I was hoping I could ask you a few questions about the scuffle involving William and Billy Doyle," she said, taking a long swallow of the drink, nearly finishing it.

"I don't recall seeing you in here…before now," he replied, eyeing her suspiciously.

"You haven't. I'm from out of town."

"Are you some kind of law?"

"No. I'm their attorney. I'm just trying to find out what happened that night. That's all. I'm not looking for any trouble."

The barkeep stepped away, filling another thimble of whiskey for a patron on the other end of the bar. He glanced in her direction as Jessie finished her drink. She turned the cup upside and waited for him to return, which he finally did a few minutes later.

"I didn't see much," he started. "There were about two dozen men at the Dice table that night. The whiskey was flowing, as it usually is. I heard shouting over the piano playing. I couldn't tell who it was, but I heard the words cheat, hustler, and fool. Then, four gun shots, followed by two more. One of the shots hit that window over there," he said, pointing behind the Dice table where a board covered the broken window. Another two hit the post next two it, one went into the beam on the ceiling, and two went into one of the men."

"What happened from there?" she asked.

"Chaos." He shook his head. "Most of the people ran out the door, except a few remaining men who stood around the table with their guns still drawn. That's when the sheriff's deputy arrived. He'd been making rounds nearby and heard the shots. Two of the remaining men were arrested."

"Do you know what their story was?"

"No, but my Dice dealer, George Young, was one of the witnesses. He saw the whole thing."

"Is that him?" she asked, nodding towards the gambling table.

"Yes."

"Do you have someone to take his place? I'd really like to talk to him."

He nodded and waved the piano player over. "I need you to cover for George for a few minutes. Send him over here," he said to the other man.

Jessie watched the dealer glance towards the bar before getting up and walking over.

"This is…" the barkeep looked at Jessie. "I don't believe I got your name."

"J. D. Homer."

"Mr. Homer is the attorney for those men who shot the other one at your table. He has some questions for you."

"Let's start with the game," Jessie said.

"Sure," he replied. "The man who was shot was losing. He'd been doing okay until those other two joined the game."

"How much had he had to drink? The man who was shot. I believe his name was Samuel Harvey."

"He had a stack of whiskey thimbles in front of him, maybe five."

"What about the other two men? William and Billy Doyle."

"One or two each. They hadn't been at the table long before the squabble began."

"Who started it?"

"The fellow who was shot. Uh…Mr. Harvey. He called the other two cheats, saying they were hustling. They called him a fool. It went back and forth, then he pointed a pistol. They told him to put the gun down, but he fired four shots in their direction. All of them missed. The two Doyle men returned fire, hitting Mr. Harvey with their shots. At that point, I ducked down, thinking everyone was going to start shooting, but the sheriff's deputy rushed in."

"What did you tell the deputy?"

"I said the fellow on the ground, Mr. Harvey, tried to shoot the other two because he thought they were hustling the game. The two Doyle men fired back, defending themselves."

There it was, the keyword Jessie was looking for: self defense.

"Did you see where the bullets hit Mr. Harvey?"

"No," he replied, shaking his head.

"Any idea what the charges were for William and Billy Doyle?"

"The deputy said something about conduct, but I didn't hear all of it."

"Thank you for talking with me," Jessie said before he went back to game. She waved the barkeep over once more. "Do you know where I can find old newspapers?"

"I believe the post keeps a copy of each paper."

"Great. I'll check with them. One more thing, is Doctor Gordon still the coroner as well?"

"John Gordon passed a couple of years ago. His son, Albert, took his place."

"Thank you," Jessie said, tipping her hat as she slid off the stool and walked outside. The warmer air was nothing like the cooler temperatures she'd left behind, which only made her yearn to be back in Boone Creek, and more so with Ellie. She'd missed her brothers over the years, but that had paled in comparison to missing her wife. That yearning feeling was something she'd felt the first time Ellie had made a trade run to Pinewood, which was something she did three to four times a year, exchanging goods with the general store there. She'd been taking the brief journey alone since her husband had passed, and despite Jessie's request to accompany her, she continued to go on her own. Every time she left, Jessie moped around until she returned.

Pushing thoughts of Ellie aside, Jessie cleared her mind and turned down Second Street, heading back towards the hotel, and the doctor's office which sat next to it in the corner of Dodd Row and Third Street.

*

Growing up poor, as the daughter of a harlot, Jessie didn't see the doctor all that often. However, Doctor Gordon's office, which took up the first floor of his small house, had been kept as though time hadn't passed. An exam table sat in the middle of the room, with a small desk pushed up into one corner, and a full bookcase next to it. Various-sized glass bottles lined a shelf on the opposite side of the room, and a wood burning stove was nearby.

"I don't see many patients here," Dr. Gordon said as he walked into the room, wiping his wire-framed spectacles on his suit jacket. He was about ten or twelve years older than Jessie, and wearing a traditional black suit with a matching vest and black tie with white polka dots. His dark brown hair was combed perfectly to the side and held in place with wax.

"I'm not here as a patient," Jessie replied. "I was hoping you could give me some information about Samuel Harvey."

"That name is unfamiliar to me," he muttered, pursing his lips in thought. "Is he a child?"

Jessie shook her head. "You pronounced him dead inside the saloon a few weeks ago."

Coroner fell under his title as the town doctor, so Dr. Gordon had seen his fair share of dead bodies, most of which had ended in a gun fight. "Yes." He nodded. "I remember him. If I'd been summoned a little faster, I might've saved that one," he sighed. "What about him?"

"Where was he shot?"

"Well...I'd have to go to my notes. I don't remember specifically, but I know he could've lived," he mumbled, going over to the bookcase. The third shelf down held two leatherback books with handwritten information filled in on the lined pages in order by date. They were the coroner's logs for the town. He grabbed the second one and opened it, flipping page after page. "What did you say his name was?"

"Harvey...Samuel Harvey."

"Ah, here it is," he exclaimed, finding the name as he ran his finger down the page. "One bullet hole in the upper left arm; no exit. One bullet hole in the right thigh; no exit."

"How did he die?"

"If you're asking for his cause of death, it was homicide, due to blood loss from multiple gunshots," he said, reading the notes.

"You said you might have saved him."

"Yes. I may have, but by the time I arrived, it was too late to stop the bleeding. I'm pretty sure his femoral artery had been nicked by the bullet."

Jessie nodded. "Thank you for the information."

"You know, I never did get your name," Dr. Gordon said.

"J. D. Homer. I'm William Doyle and Billy Doyle's attorney," she replied.

"I see," he mumbled as she left.

*

Jessie wanted to go back and check on her brothers, but she knew better than to go near the sheriff's office again. If there truly was a bounty on her head, she needed to steer clear of the law, or anyone who might recognize her.

As she stepped out of the doctor's office, she spotted a woman standing on the upper balcony of the brothel, looking her way. Even from that distance, there was no mistaking the ample bosom, and curvy hips of 'Good' Gertie Henry. The woman tilted her head to the side, almost as if she was trying to place Jessie. She quickly lowered her chin and headed off in the opposite direction, blending in with the people on the sidewalk as she disappeared from sight. If there was one person who would recognize her and turn her in for the bounty money, it was Gertie.

Her harlot mother had been the last person she'd expected to see. From the looks of her, her whoring lifestyle hadn't changed. Jessie hadn't gotten close enough to see her face, but she was sure it was aged well beyond its years.

Sighing inwardly, she pushed away the thoughts of a woman she'd never respected, and focused on her brothers as she walked inside the hotel. "Any messages for me?" she asked, stopping at the desk. "Room 204, J. D. Homer."

The man across from her checked his log book. "No, sir," he replied, shaking his head.

Without the sheriff's report, she had no idea what the official charges were, or how to go about getting them dropped. *Newspapers*, she thought, remembering she still needed to get copies of the old newspapers. She turned and headed back outside, walking in the direction of the post. Her mind drifted back to her conversation with Dr. Gordon. She wasn't a lawyer and had no legal knowledge, other than what she'd needed to do her job as the Town Marshal in Boone Creek. Colorado was still a territory, so their laws were slightly different from the actual states.

*

The Castor Valley post had done a fairly decent job of archiving the town newspaper for their records. Jessie was able to secure copies of each of the three weeks since the shooting. After having a roast beef and potato dinner in the hotel dining area, she headed up to her room and removed her suit jacket, tie, and vest. It had also felt good to get that itchy mustache off her face. She sat down at the small desk and began perusing the paper for articles about the shooting.

Ironically, two days after it had happened, the paper released their issue for the week. She found what she was looking for on page two.

Gunfight at the Cattleman's Saloon, was the article title. She quickly read over the short passage. *Samuel Harvey died from his wounds after a gunfight with William and Billy Doyle in the saloon. William and Billy claimed to have shot him in self defense, and were arrested for disorderly conduct.*

Jessie had already known all of this. She set the paper aside and went to the next one.

The two men arrested in the Cattleman's Saloon gunfight, William Doyle and Billy Doyle, identified as members of the Eldorado Gang, a deadly trio of murdering and thieving outlaws. Eye witness statements seem to paint a different picture of what happened that night in the saloon. The sheriff stated, 'The charges have been changed from disorderly conduct to murder because we believe the Eldorado Gang was here to rob the saloon, and perhaps the bank. Mr. Harvey had seen them on a wanted poster and pointed them out in the crowd.'

Further down the page, she saw the wanted poster with a poor drawing of her face on it.

Jessie Henry, outlaw and leader of the Eldorado Gang. Wanted for murder, and thievery. Armed and dangerous. Blonde hair/green eyes. Goes by La Diabla. Last seen in Mexico. $500 reward. Wanted: Alive.

Jessie shook her head as she flipped the paper over and moved onto the last one.

William Doyle and Billy Doyle of the Eldorado Gang headed to trial for the murder of Samuel Harvey. Both men are set to stand trial in two weeks. The sheriff has stated that the case against the men is strong, and we will see them hang for the pain they have caused the families of those whom they killed while conniving with Jessie Henry, the leader of the Eldorado Gang.

"We never killed anyone," she said, reading back over the article. "*We* didn't…but *I* did," she mumbled as an image of Joe flashed through her head. "How the hell could the sheriff here know anything about that?"

Knowing the sheriff knew more about her than she thought, Jessie couldn't chance crossing paths with him and was glad he'd been unavailable when she'd seen her brothers. Still, Joe had rarely spoke of family, so she had no idea who the sheriff was. The last time she'd lived there, the sheriff's name was Rutherford Martin. "I don't think I ever heard Joe mention Sheriff Martin. In fact, I'm sure he didn't even know who he was."

She searched each newspaper, looking for the name of the current sheriff, but found nothing. She quickly put her vest, tie, and jacket back on. Then, she re-applied her mustache, and pulled her hat down low.

*

The man at the lobby desk of the hotel was the same one she'd seen the night before when checking in. He gave a polite nod as Jessie passed by on her way out. There were about as many people out and about on the streets as there had been when she'd arrived during the night. She weaved through them, keeping a steady pace, but not moving oddly enough to attract attention to herself.

When she reached the saloon, Jessie pulled the door open and meandered over to the same stool she'd occupied that morning.

"Back again?" the barkeep asked, filling her a thimble of whiskey when she tipped her hat in his direction.

"Is Rutherford Martin still the sheriff?" she asked, taking a long swallow.

"He retired about two years ago. Fred Clarence took his place."

Jessie's chest tightened. *Son of a bitch!*

"You okay?" he asked.

"Yeah," she muttered.

"That's him back there," the barkeep said, tilting his head towards the Dice game.

Jessie turned enough to see the man in the dark suit with an ascot tie, gambler hat, and thick sideburns. His hair was the same gray as Joe's had been.

"Does he come in here often?"

"Most nights."

"Is he working or gambling."

"Little of both, I guess."

Jessie wanted to pull her hidden pistol and shoot him herself for using her brothers to lure her there as a revenge ploy for something he knew nothing about. She wasn't sure what he'd do or how far he'd go, but one thing was certain, he was looking for her. *I'm not letting you hurt my brothers, you crooked son of a bitch!* She thought as she walked out, disappearing within the locals in the street.

*

The next morning, Jessie went straight to the post and sent Ellie another cryptic message:

Worse than I thought. Attacker's brother is sheriff. After JH head for murder. Not sure how to save boys. Trial soon. Turning in bounty only way. Goodbye Love.

She paid the fee for the words and waited for it to be sent and destroyed. Then, she blended back in with the locals as she headed back to the hotel.

EIGHT

Boone Creek, Colorado Territory

"Mrs. Henry," A boy called, stepping into the General Trade.

Ellie was assisting a customer, so she held her hand up to him. She watched as he leaned a little closer to the freshly baked honey biscuits that were sitting on the counter near the register. She'd made them for Bert and Molly and had planned to take them over when the store closed.

The boy sniffed the air, but had kept his hands in his pockets the entire time he waited for Mr. Brown to finish picking out a scented candle as a gift for his wife. As soon as the man left, Ellie walked over to him.

"May I help you?" she asked.

"I have two telegrams for you," he replied, handing them to her.

"Thank you," she said with a big smile, knowing they were from Jessie. She opened the register and handed him a bit coin.

He said a polite thank you and moved to leave, but took one last sniff of the air.

"Would you like a biscuit?"

"They smell wonderful."

"According to Marshal Henry, they taste even better. Go on, get yourself one." She nodded towards the basket.

He smiled brightly and pulled the cloth covering back, grabbing one from the top before covering them back up. "Thank you, Mrs. Henry."

"You're welcome," she replied, holding onto the two small pieces of paper. As soon as he was gone, she read the messages. Ellie had no idea who J.D. Homer was, but she was sure they were from Jessie. The cryptic wording threw her off at first, but the more she read over them, the more she felt like Jessie was in danger. "Oh, Jessie. Please be okay," she mumbled, holding the messages to her chest.

It was close to dark, and near time for the store to close, so Ellie went ahead and locked up for the night, and headed down the street with the messages in her skirt pocket. She'd thought about showing them to Bert when she dropped off the biscuits, but she wasn't sure he'd be able to do much. Besides, she was pretty sure Jessie hadn't told him exactly why she'd had to leave town to begin with. In fact, she wasn't sure Jessie had told the person she was on the way to see either, but she had to take a chance. She feared for Jessie's life.

*

A light was on upstairs in the mayor's house, indicating he was in his office, working late. After a loud knock got his attention, Mayor Montgomery rushed down to see who was calling on him. He pulled the door open, gasping when he saw the woman standing across from him. "Ellie?" he questioned. "Come in. Come in," he said, hurriedly waving her inside. "Is everything okay?"

"Mayor Montgomery, I wouldn't bother, certainly not in the evening hours, if it wasn't important. I received two telegrams from Jessie not long ago, and they have me worried. I'm afraid she's in danger."

"What do you mean?" he asked, grabbing the papers she handed him. He read over the odd messages. "Who is J.D. Homer?"

"Jessie. She's using a fake name."

His brow scrunched in surprise. "Why would she do that?"

"I'm pretty sure the $500 prize means a bounty on her head, so that probably has something to do with it," Ellie replied, shaking her head. "I knew going there was a bad idea. She even said it herself, but her brothers mean so much to her, she couldn't let them hang."

"Wait...what? I thought she was going to help a family member who was sick, get their affairs in order."

Ellie shook her head.

"Son of a bitch!" he growled.

"She's in trouble, and she needs your help."

"I don't even know where she is!" he spat.

"I do, and if they find out she's there, she's going to hang right beside her brothers."

Mayor Montgomery shook his head in frustration.

"After everything she's done for you and this town...I'm asking you to help her," Ellie pleaded.

Being lied to made him madder than a wet hen, but he couldn't let something happen to her, she was like family.

"Let's go up to my office. I want the truth. You can start at the beginning," he said, escorting her up the stairs.

*

Ellie told the mayor the same story Jessie had relayed to her about her childhood, the cattleman, and finding her brothers, as well as starting and ending the outlaw gang. He was surprised, but not shocked. He'd had a feeling Jessie's life had been tumultuous when he'd hired her, but over the past two years, he'd seen the hardnosed, gritty outlaw chip away some of her rigid exterior.

"I'm not a law officer, but I'm pretty sure there's a hidden message in the telegrams," Ellie said, reading over them again.

"I have a feeling you're right. It sounds to me like she might sacrifice herself to save her brothers."

"I think so, too. We can't let her do that. They'll surely hang her," Ellie cried.

"Let me figure this out tonight. I'll be at your store when it opens in the morning."

"Okay," Ellie agreed.

"Here, let me walk you home," he said, grabbing his jacket.

"Mayor, I'm perfectly capable of seeing myself home."

"Oh, Mrs. Henry, I have no doubt that's true. However, if something were to happen to you, I wouldn't want to face our Town Marshal. It's best I look out for you."

Ellie smiled, knowing he was simply being honest.

*

After pacing the floor, then tossing and turning in the bed, Ellie found herself sitting by the window, staring out at the stars as she waited for the sun to come up so she could open the store. Having not slept made her dread the long day ahead, but her thoughts were on Jessie.

She watched the orange and red rays crest the mountain in the distance, slowly bringing a new day to life. *Please be okay, Jessie,* she thought as she wiped away a tear and dressed in a crème colored blouse with light blue stripes and a darker blue walking skirt. After tying her boots, she brushed out her wavy, brown hair, and braided it into one long strand that she twisted up into a bun, finishing it with bobby pins that held the hair in place. She glanced at Jessie's side of the bed, before rushing down the stairs to open the store.

"Good morning," Bert called from the sidewalk in front of the marshal's office, which sat nearly directly across from her building on Main Street Curve. "Molly should be stopping by this morning to thank you in person for the biscuits!"

"Great. I look forward to seeing her and Eddie!" she yelled back as she pulled her daily specials, chalkboard-sign out onto the sidewalk and began updating it for the day.

No sooner had she finished, when Molly walked up, pushing the baby buggy.

"You must give me that recipe. I've tried over and over to make those darn biscuits, but they never come out the same," Molly chided with a smile as she followed Ellie inside.

"It's simple. Double the buttermilk," Ellie laughed. "As for the honey jam, well, it starts out as apple mush, like you'd make for an apple jam. I add in enough honey to sweeten it and mask the apple flavor. Then, I mix it forever and let it thicken for a day or two," she added, reaching down to play with the baby.

Molly nodded, taking a mental note. "How are things with Jessie being gone?"

"I miss her terribly," Ellie sighed. "In fact, I got a telegram from her yesterday. It sounds like she's in over her head out there. I'm thinking of going to help her out."

"If you need help with the store, I don't mind me looking after it for you."

"What about Eddie? I can't do that to you."

"Oh, he'll be fine."

"I wouldn't want the knitting ladies to speak ill of you," Ellie said sarcastically.

Molly laughed. "You're starting to sound like Jessie."

Ellie smiled and shook her head. "If you're serious, and don't think it will interfere with the baby…then yes, I could certainly use the help. I'm not sure how long I'll be gone. It could be a week or two."

"I'll be fine. You go get packed while I run over and discuss it with Bert," Molly said. She turned and headed out the door with the buggy, and Mayor Montgomery walked in.

"Good, you're here. I'm about to go pack a bag. Molly is watching the store."

"Where are you off to?" he asked.

"I assume we're going to help Jessie. That's why you're here."

"*I* am…yes."

"I'm going with you," she replied stubbornly.

"Mrs. Henry, I can't take you along," he sighed, tapping his hat against his leg.

"And why not?"

"It's completely unethical."

"Mayor Montgomery, either you escort me, or I'll go it alone. It's your choice. Now, if you'll excuse me, I need to go pack a bag."

He stared after her as she rushed up the stairs. "Jessie Henry, I'm liable to hang you myself," he mumbled, shaking his head as he walked out of the store. He had no other choice, but to bring Ellie along. He couldn't risk leaving her behind to travel by herself.

NINE

Mayor Montgomery didn't have to go far to find what he was looking for. "Get your lazy ass up," he said, kicking the boots of the man sitting on the sidewalk, leaning back against the side of the Rustler's Den Saloon.

"What?" he mumbled, falling over in a drunken stupor.

"Damn it, Otis!" he growled, storming off and heading into the saloon.

"Afternoon, Mayor," Elmer said with a nod.

"I need a big, strong cup of coffee. In fact, make it two."

"Sure. Give me a few minutes," Elmer replied before disappearing to the back.

Mayor Montgomery sat on a stool, ignoring the patrons, as he waited for the barkeep to return. The few people who walked in, went unnoticed as he mentally went over the route he'd outlined for the trip down to Texas.

"Here you go," Elmer said, sliding two steaming cups of coffee across the bar.

The mayor shook the thoughts from his head. "I also need a cup of water," he said. "And it's to go, so charge me for the mugs. Put it all on my tab."

Elmer nodded. "You're going to need help carrying these. How far are you going?"

"Just around the corner."

Elmer walked out from behind the bar and grabbed the coffee mugs while the mayor carried the water. He followed as the mayor led the way around the side of the saloon to where Otis was slumped over.

Mayor Montgomery tossed the water on Otis and kicked his boots. "Wake up!" he yelled.

Otis jerked to the side and began wiping the water from his face.

Elmer gulped and took a step back.

"I'll take those," the mayor said, grabbing the mugs. He looked back at Otis, then at the barkeep. "Don't ask," he said.

Elmer nodded and quickly headed back into the saloon.

"Why the hell did you pour water on me?" Otis growled.

"Because I need you to get up. Here, drink this. It'll help you sober up." Mayor Montgomery handed him one of the mugs.

"What for?" Otis mumbled, taking a sip.

"Someone needs our help."

"Who?"

"It doesn't matter. Drink both of these and meet me at my office in twenty minutes." He handed him the other mug and began to walk away. Turning back, he said, "And Otis, if you don't show up, I'll drag you behind my horse," he added.

*

Otis was a few minutes late, but he still managed to make it to his destination. Mayor Montgomery gave him an old suit to wear, and escorted him to the bath house to wash the smell off. From there, he took him over to Muddy Joe to get a fresh shave, and trim his scraggly hair. After that, they headed down Main Street, towards the stage.

"Are you going to tell me where we're going?"

"Texas."

"Oh, no I'm not," Otis barked, stopping in the middle of the sidewalk. The coffee had woken him up, but he was still a little tipsy.

"Oh, yes you are. Come on."

"I said I'd never go back to that state."

"Well, you lied to yourself, Otis. Now, come on. The stage is waiting for us."

"This better be well worth my time," Otis growled, stumbling slightly as he began walking again.

"I'll make sure you're compensated generously when we return," the mayor huffed. *Damn you, Jessie Henry,* he thought, shaking his head.

*

Ellie was already in the stage when Mayor Montgomery arrived. She glanced sideways at the man standing next to him, surprised to see he'd cleaned up the town drunk and brought him along. "I was unaware anyone else would be traveling with us," she stated as they climbed inside.

"Otis is coming along to help me with a matter," the mayor said, not giving away too much information. He was well aware of the animosity between Otis and the Town Marshal, and the least Otis knew about where they were going and what they were doing, the better.

"I see," she replied.

"What's she doing here? I'm not going anywhere with the Lady Law," he spat, looking all around for Jessie.

"She's not accompanying me on this trip," Ellie stated.

"Good," he mumbled, sitting on the velvet-covered, cushioned bench across from her.

Mayor Montgomery climbed in behind him and sat down next to Ellie. They both watched as Otis stretched out along the bench on his back and put his hat over his face. He was sound asleep, snoring like a warthog, before the coach even left. Ellie shook her head in disgust.

"Let him sleep it off," the mayor whispered.

"I still don't see why you brought him."

"We'll need him. Trust me," he replied, looking out the window as the coach began the journey over to the next town.

Ellie nodded, but she wasn't sure she believed him. She turned her attention to the window, watching the open range go by as the coach bumped along the trail. She missed Jessie dearly, and no matter how hard she tried, she couldn't shake the thought of something bad happening to her. Jessie was a keen woman, but she was also stubborn as a mule. When she set her mind on something, she followed through. Ellie said a silent prayer for God to watch over her wife and keep her safe.

*

The stage ride to Red Rock had taken a little more than a full day, but by using two drivers and adding two extra horses, making it a four horse cart, they'd gotten there much quicker than the usual two day ride.

Ellie looked around at the town. Not much had changed since she'd come through a little over four years ago with her husband, Cornelius Fray.

"The train station is this way," Mayor Montgomery said, leading the two of them down the sidewalk. It had been some time since he'd last been there as well.

Otis trudged along behind them. He'd begun to sober up on the trail, and the mayor pulled a bottle of whiskey from his bag, handing it to the drunk to keep him at bay.

"We need three tickets on the Santa Fe Rail Line to El Paso," the mayor said, stepping up to the ticket window.

"Will that be first, second, or third class, sir?"

"First."

"I don't have any sleeper coaches available, but I do have three seats together in a first class coach near the dining coach. Will that be okay?"

"Sure," the mayor said, handing him two double eagles to pay for the tickets.

"Next train leaves in one hour."

"Horace, I believe there is a restaurant over on the next street. We should have enough time to have lunch," Ellie said, calling him by his first name.

He furrowed his brow and quickly grabbed the tickets.

"I apologize, Mayor—" she said.

"Nonsense. The least amount of people who know who we are, the better. In fact, you should probably drop the Henry name once we get there. We certainly don't need to draw attention to ourselves. If they're looking for her, they're looking for that name as well."

"I agree. I'll go back to using Fray."

He nodded. "Come on, I'm famished." The two of them began to walk away, before he turned around and yelled for Otis to follow. "We're going to have to sober him up at some point."

"I still don't understand why he's with us."

"You will," he replied.

TEN

Castor Valley, Texas

Jessie hadn't received a return telegram from Ellie. Then again, she hadn't expected her to reply. Her brothers' trial was set to take place in three days, and she still wasn't completely sure what to do, or who to trust. The sheriff supposedly had several witnesses against them. However, most of the names weren't available to her, and those she did get, seemed to have disappeared. She'd come down to what seemed to be her only option, turning herself in to save them, when an odd telegram was delivered to her.

Holdfast. Arriving Tuesday.
-Horace

She contemplated the cryptic message as she ate dinner, still surprised that the mayor of Castor Valley was on his way to her. Then again, she knew Ellie would go to him for help. Judging by the timing of the telegram, which had been sent from El Paso, the mayor would be arriving the next day. The only problem was, Jessie had no idea how he was going to help her free her brothers.

After her meal, she walked over to the livery. Homer the horse was long gone, having either been sold off or perhaps perished from old age, but the stables looked as if time hadn't passed. Images of her childhood flashed through her mind as she walked around. At the age of ten, she'd begun working for pennies, cleaning stalls. It wasn't the most exciting job, but it got her out of the brothel, and shoveling shit was far better than listening to whores with their guests all afternoon. Each day after school, she'd go to the livery until just before dark. She'd return to the brothel to eat whatever scraps had been left for her in the kitchen, then she'd sit up on the roof, studying the stars until she was about to fall asleep. A space in the house attic had been cleared, with a mattress on the floor for her to sleep on. This way her mother could work and keep overnight guests. It also gave Jessie access to the roof through a vent hatch.

"Are you in need of a horse?" a young man asked, pulling Jessie from her unpleasant memories.

She simply shook her head and exited the building, heading for the back door of the nearby saloon, hoping a couple of glasses of whiskey would wash away the past she'd tried so hard to forget.

*

"Haven't seen you in a couple of days," the bartender asked, holding up a whiskey bottle.

Jessie nodded. "Been working on my case," she replied, sitting on a vacant stool.

"I don't think those young men stand a chance, I'm afraid."

"Why is that?"

"Sheriff Clarence has been after that gang for some time now. He's busted up several outlaw groups that have passed through, hoping they were who he was looking for, or at least knew where to find them. I'm surprised they even came here to begin with."

Jessie pulled a cigar from her vest pocket and lit it with a match from the holder on the bar. She knew why her brothers were there. They were looking for her and had no idea the crooked sheriff was after them in a bounty hunt fueled by vengeance. "Wrong place at the wrong time, I suppose," she said.

The barkeep shrugged. "You want another?" he asked, nodding towards her empty glass.

Jessie pushed it over to him.

"Are you looking for some company tonight?" a woman asked, slithering up against her side.

Jessie pushed her away, politely refusing before the harlot found the gun tucked into the back of her pants. She quickly drank the glass of whiskey and set a trade dollar coin underneath it. Then, she tipped her hat towards the barkeep, who had walked down to the other end, before leaving. The more time she spent around the locals, the more they would be inclined to know her. That simply couldn't happen.

ELEVEN

San Antonio, Texas

Ellie and Mayor Montgomery had just arrived by train with a half-drunken Otis in tow. The mayor asked Ellie to go book the stage while he took Otis to the barber for a shave and a bath. They met back up an hour later in the restaurant near the stage office, where they forced Otis to drink coffee.

"We have to sober him up. He needs to be on his toes when we arrive," Mayor Montgomery mumbled. "How long is the stage ride?"

"Half a day at most."

The mayor chewed the edge of his thick, white mustache.

"If he needs to be sober, then why did you let him drink so much?" Ellie whispered a little harshly.

"Because he's an ornery bastard as it is. Could you imagine him sober for this entire trip?"

Ellie shook her head. "I would've tossed him off the train myself," she muttered.

"Exactly."

"Tell me why he's here. He's more of a burden than beneficial."

"He's a Texas lawyer."

Ellie's brow furrowed as her face scrunched.

"Well, he *was*…I should say."

"When was this?"

"Several years ago, I believe."

Ellie stared in utter shock at the drunkard as he sat at the table beside them, sipping coffee and eating breakfast. "What happened?" she asked.

"No idea, but I'm pretty sure it's the reason he drinks his life away."

"You honestly think he's going to help Jessie? I'm pretty sure he'd rather walk all the way back to Boone Creek, and if I know Jessie, she's not going to be happy either."

Mayor Montgomery shrugged. "He's all we have. They'll either work together, or kill each other."

She nodded in agreement. "He'll help or he won't be coming back with us. That I can assure you," she replied, watching him eat.

*

The stagecoach had red, plush, velvet seats and gold trim, and was similar to the one they'd ridden in to Red Rock from Castor Valley, although it seemed to bounce a little less on the trail. Otis fell asleep quickly. Ellie and Mayor Montgomery were nearly out of small talk from the long trip, but found it easy to discuss the sights around them as they traveled on. The mayor had never been to Texas, and Ellie had only passed through by train on her way to Tombstone from Dodge City. In fact, it had been the same rail they'd taken down to El Paso from Red Rock.

TWELVE

Castor Valley, Texas

Jessie stood across from the stage office, watching intently as the coach arrived in town, trotting slowly down Central Street. She had mixed feelings about Mayor Montgomery coming to Castor Valley, where he'd more than likely be subject to her entire past.

"Whoa!" the driver yelled, pulling back on the reins, bringing the carriage to a stop along the side of the office building. He climbed down, retrieved the luggage bags from the roof, then opened the side door.

Jessie saw a man climb out, handing the driver an obvious tip, before turning with his hand held out to assist another passenger. She recognized Mayor Montgomery by his mustache, and tall, slender build. He helped a woman, who exited and stood next to him. She was wearing a dark blue dress suit with black velvet trim. Her light brown hair was braided and wrapped up in a bun, under a small black hat. Jessie strained her eyes, trying to see in the dim lighting. The sun had almost set, and the lamplighters were already hard at work, lighting up the streets. *Ellie…* she thought, feeling her chest tighten with excitement. *What is she doing here?* Turning her eyes back to the carriage, she saw a third passenger get out, closing the door behind him. She'd never seen him clean, but she could make out that scrawny frame anywhere, even in a suit that was a size too big. "Otis? What the hell?" she whispered.

"Where are we supposed to go?" Ellie asked, grabbing her bag.

"I have no idea. I posted ahead, letting her know I was arriving," Mayor Montgomery said, looking around. "Excuse me, sir. Do you know where the hotel is?" he asked the driver.

"It's over on Dodd Row," he said, pointing. "That's First Street right there, but it's a little shady this time of night," he added, looking at Ellie. "If you go up to Second Street, it runs into Dodd Row. Take a left and you'll see the hotel down on your right."

"Thank you," Mayor Montgomery replied. "This way," he called to his companions.

"Now that we've arrived, are you going to tell me why you dragged me all the way down here?" Otis mumbled.

"A friend is in legal trouble," the mayor answered.

"I don't practice law anymore," Otis grumbled.

"You still remember everything, don't you?"

Otis folded his arms and gritted his teeth. "You owe me for this."

"I know. I know," the mayor sighed, shaking his head. He was starting to wonder if bringing Otis had been a bad idea after all.

As soon as they turned down Second Street, which ran alongside the saloon, a man stepped out of the shadows in front of them. "Are you looking for the hotel?" he asked.

Ellie scrunched her brow at the familiarity. She tried to place the man, feeling like she'd seen him before. She knew she'd certainly heard his voice.

Mayor Montgomery was about to ask him to step away when the man removed his hat and pulled the side of his mustache back.

"Oh, my God!" Ellie squealed, lurching into Jessie's arms.

Jessie put her mustache back and slid her hat on, before wrapping her arms around her wife. "Oh, how I've missed you," she whispered, kissing her cheek.

"Lady Law!" Otis growled. "I'm not helping her!"

"Keep it down!" Jessie and Mayor Montgomery both hissed.

"Why is he here?" Jessie asked.

The mayor held his hand out to Jessie as Ellie stepped aside. "He's a Texas lawyer."

"Not anymore," Otis grumbled.

"You didn't have to come here...any of you," Jessie said, shaking his hand.

"Yes. Yes, we did. I'm not happy about being lied to, but I can't let something happen to you."

"Well, I can! I'd rather kiss a rattlesnake than help her with anything," Otis spat.

A loud SMACK got all of their attention as Ellie lost control, slapping Otis across the face. "She's done nothing to you except lock your sorry butt in jail when you get drunk and show out around town. If it wasn't for her, someone probably would've shot you by now," she said through clenched teeth. "She needs your help!"

"I agree with her. Now, get over yourself and get to work. I'm not paying you for standing here acting a fool," Mayor Montgomery said.

"I want double the pay," Otis grumbled, chomping at the bit a little more.

"Fine."

"We should get you all checked into the hotel. We can talk in my room," Jessie said. "I'm going by J.D. Homer, an attorney from out of town," she added.

"I've been using the Fray name since we left, and he's been using his name without the title," Ellie replied, nodding towards the mayor.

"You can switch to Homer. There's no reason why you can't still be my wife." Jessie smiled softly.

"What's with all the secrecy? And why you are parading around as a man? Isn't it bad enough you're married to a woman?" Otis muttered.

"There's a bounty on my head," Jessie answered, staring at the drunkard like she was about to knock him silly.

Otis looked at the mayor and shook his head.

"Come on. Let's get out of the street," Mayor Montgomery said, urging everyone along.

*

Jessie had introduced the three of them to the man at the hotel desk, as his wife and colleagues. Otis and Mayor Montgomery shared a room with twin beds, down the hall from Jessie's room, mainly so that the mayor could keep an eye on him. Once everyone was settled, they all met in Jessie's room. She removed her mustache, making her look more like herself, which Ellie was happy about.

"The sheriff here has a beef with me," she began. "He's corrupt and unlawful. He's holding two members of my old gang, and planning to hang them, based on fake charges."

"Let me guess, he's trying to bring you to justice, too. Which, I believe is what sheriffs are supposed to do with outlaws," Otis said sarcastically.

"I killed his brother," she replied.

Otis folded his arms and looked sideways at the mayor. "I'm not defending no outlaw murderer," he huffed.

Ellie raised her hand to slap him again, but Jessie grabbed it. "Yes, I've killed people, but I have never shot first, and they were hardly innocent. The man I killed, forced himself on me. I was able to get away, but he tried to kill me. I shot him while trying to defend myself," she sighed, growing tired of reliving that horrific night over and over. "Look, the gang dissolved two years ago. I went to Boone Creek to start my life over, and from what I've found out, William and Billy have hung around the area, hoping I'd return someday. None of us are outlaws anymore."

"To start the gang back up?" Otis questioned.

"No." Jessie shook her head. "They don't even know they're really my little brothers. I happened to run into them not long after their mother died. I realized we all shared the same father, but I kept it to myself. I was a loner back then. I tried to keep them from following me down the wrong path, but they did it anyway. They were just kids, and now they're set to die for something that had nothing to do with them."

"What are they actually charged with?" Otis asked.

"Murder, but it was originally disorderly conduct. It changed once the sheriff found out who they were."

"What did they do?"

"An argument with an intoxicated man, over a dice game, got out of hand. He drew his gun, shooting around four shots at them before they returned fire. From the statement they gave me, they didn't intend to kill him."

"And you believe them?"

"I taught William and Billy how to handle a gun with their eyes closed. If they'd wanted him dead, he would've been shot in the chest and head, not the arm and leg."

"What about the coroner's report? Have you seen it?"

"I spoke with him. He reported it as a homicide."

"General? Not justified, or felonious?"

"Yes."

"Did he mention murder?"

"No. He just said homicide, but he did say that he could've been saved. So, from looking at the wounds, he could tell the intent wasn't to kill them. At least, that's what I got from talking with him."

Otis nodded. "I haven't practiced law in over ten years. I'm not sure how much help I can be."

"I only met with the boys once, and the sheriff wasn't there, so I didn't see the actual reports. I didn't find out who he was until a few days later, and I haven't been back."

"I'll start there," he said.

*

As soon as the mayor and Otis left the room, Jessie pulled Ellie into her arms, kissing her tenderly.

"I wasn't sure you'd be happy to see me," Ellie said, leaning back to look in her eyes.

"Truth be told, I wasn't. I don't know how this is all going to end, but I'm glad you're here. This place isn't home to me, but you…this," she said, referring to their position. "Feels like home."

"Mayor Montgomery tried to leave me behind, but I threatened to go alone. I couldn't let you do something stupid, and I felt…" She began to cry. "I felt like you might turn yourself in to save them."

"I have to do something. I can't let that son of a bitch hang them," Jessie sighed, lowering her arms and taking a small step back.

"When I shot Willie, I was free, but I lived in fear. When Corny was murdered, I was sad, but I grew strong and moved on. Then, you came into my life and turned everything upside down. I'd never had such a strong emotional and physical connection with anyone. You scared me and fascinated me at the same time. I wanted to hate you, but I knew I loved you. Becoming your wife was the last thing I thought would ever happen, but it's been the best part of my life. I can't lose you, Jessie," Ellie cried.

"You're not going to. I'm right here, and I'm not going anywhere," Jessie murmured, pulling her in close.

The feeling of Jessie's arms around her always had a soothing affect on Ellie. She looked at her wife and smiled at the beautiful green eyes that tugged at her heart.

"I'm glad you don't still hate me," Jessie teased, reaching out to wipe away her tears. "I love you more than anything, Ellie," she whispered, kissing her softly. "Everything will be fine," she added when their lips parted.

Ellie nodded, believing she was right. "You said you saw them. How are they doing?" she asked, thinking about Jessie's brothers.

"I did, a couple of days ago. I didn't recognize either of them. They don't look good at all, but neither does anyone else who is locked up in jail."

"Hopefully, Otis can figure out what to do and get them out."

"You really think he can? He's a grouchy, old drunk. How the hell did Mayor Montgomery even know he was a lawyer?"

Ellie shrugged. "He didn't even tell my why Otis was with us until we were almost here."

"This dress is beautiful, by the way. I forgot to mention that you took my breath away when you stepped out of that carriage," Jessie admitted, changing the subject as she kissed her again.

"I borrowed it from Molly," Ellie replied, running her hand down the front of Jessie's suit.

Jessie began unbuttoning the front of the dress top as she slid her mouth over to Ellie's neck, tracing delicate kisses.

Slowly, piece by piece, their clothing was discarded until they were naked, facing one another. Together, they tugged the blanket back on the bed and sat down, meeting in the middle. Jessie pulled Ellie into her arms and rolled on top of her.

"Oh, how I've missed you…and this," Ellie murmured.

"I haven't been gone that long."

"One night without you beside me in our bed was uneasy, but after a couple of days it became downright lonely. I certainly don't sleep without my bed clothes when you're not home."

"So, I've spoiled you, then."

Ellie shrugged and looked away, trying to hide her smile.

Jessie grinned. "I think I have a remedy for that," she mumbled, kissing her way down the creamy skin of Ellie's chest.

Ellie pushed up into her, thrusting her left breast closer to Jessie's mouth. However, Jessie avoided her breasts all together, and ran her mouth up and down her body, tracing delicate kisses that left Ellie panting and wanting more.

"Kiss me *there*, Jessie," she breathed heavily.

Obliging her yearning wife, Jessie moved between her legs, sliding her tongue through Ellie's wetness.

"Oh, yes!" Ellie called.

"The entire hotel is going to hear you through these paper thin walls," Jessie chided softly.

"Don't stop!" Ellie puffed in the throes of passion. Her body was rigid. Blood raced through her veins at horrendous speed as her heart pumped like it was about to jump out of her chest.

After a few more passes with her tongue, Jessie slipped her fingers inside of Ellie, sending her careening over the edge of the massive peak that had built up inside of her.

"Oh my God!" Ellie cried out before her body went limp. Her skin was warm and wet with sweat, and her chest heaved up and down from her heavy breathing.

Jessie crawled up next to her, gathering Ellie's spent body into her arms. She kissed her hairline at the top of her forehead.

"I need to touch you," Ellie whispered as her body slowly came back to reality.

Jessie flattened onto her back, allowing Ellie full access to her.

Starting slowly, Ellie ran her hand up and down Jessie's smooth skin from the top of her shoulder, across her torso, and down her thigh, avoiding the spot she knew she was needed most.

Jessie's breathing picked up as Ellie's finger inched closer and closer to her throbbing center. She knew Ellie had to explore her every time they made love, making it like the first time all over again.

Running her hands over another woman's body, feeling the softness of her tender skin, was something Ellie knew she would never get used to. She could spend all night just touching Jessie, which would probably drive her to the point of craziness with desire.

Ellie finally adjusted her hand and moved in closer, making lazy passes with her fingers over Jessie's wetness.

"Mmm…" Jessie mumbled breathlessly as Ellie began making precise circles, pressing firmer. Her back arched and her hips rose to meet each pass until she shivered with a thundering release that left her feeling like she was outside of her own body.

Ellie eased her fingers away. She was already cuddled against Jessie's side, so she leaned in, kissing her softly.

"I love you," Jessie whispered, rolling her head to the side to look into her eyes.

"I love you, too," Ellie smiled.

THIRTEEN

Otis was sitting in the hotel restaurant with Mayor Montgomery, drinking coffee and eating breakfast, when Ellie and Jessie appeared. Ellie had a rather sheepish look on her face, hoping no one had heard them the night before, but Jessie's train of thought went right to Otis when she noticed his hand trembling slightly from alcohol withdrawal.

"Are you going to be able to keep that in check?" she asked, nodding towards the wavering cup in his hand.

"Do you want me to help you, or not?" he muttered.

Mayor Montgomery cleared his throat in attempt to get the attention of the two of them before they went at each other for the umpteenth time. "What's your plan for the day, Otis?"

"I'm going to the sheriff's office to talk with the men, and hopefully see the report from the night they were arrested, as well as the new one from when the charges were added. I'm assuming you've met with the barkeep at the saloon, correct?" he said, looking at Jessie.

"Yes. He wasn't much of a witness, however, the Dice dealer saw the whole thing."

"And you spoke with him already?"

Jessie nodded.

"There really isn't much left to do, except view the reports. I may see the coroner again. Were there other witnesses that you know of?"

"Yes, but I couldn't track down any of them," Jessie stated.

Finishing his last sip of coffee, Otis set the cup down, feeling somewhat better as the hidden booze began to flow through his body. He wasn't drunk by any means, but going sober cold turkey had made him become extremely ill, so the mayor slipped him a little whiskey in his coffee to put him back on an even keel.

"I'll meet you back here in a few hours," Otis said, standing up from the table.

Jessie stood to go along.

"The desk attendant drew me a map of the town, so I should be okay to find my way around. There's no need to risk you getting discovered. Although, $500 would feel nice in my pockets," he said.

"Try not to get yourself locked up next to them," Jessie sneered, sitting back down. She watched Otis wave her off as he walked away. "He's had a drink, hasn't he?"

"He woke up vomiting all over the room. I had to do something. We couldn't very well have him getting sick all over the sheriff's office," Mayor Montgomery said. "I gave him enough to quell the shakes and nausea, but he's far from inebriation."

Jessie sighed. "How are things back home?" she asked, trying to get her mind off the mess she was in.

"Bert's doing okay, if that's what you're asking. He's learned a lot in the past two years, and certainly come a long way. I wouldn't have left him alone if I didn't feel comfortable doing so."

"So, let me get this straight, he's filling in for both of us?" Jessie asked, slightly surprised.

"Well…no one really knows I'm gone…so he shouldn't have a problem…but yes."

"That's a hell of a lot of trust to put in a deputy's hands," Jessie mumbled, thinking out loud.

"I didn't have much of a choice. If the town goes up in flames in the five or six days that I'm gone, then I probably shouldn't have been the mayor to begin with."

Jessie nodded in agreement. That was sort of the way she felt about leaving herself. If she'd trained Bert right, then he should've been fine while she was gone.

*

Morning quickly turned into afternoon. The great state of Texas took a lot longer to cool down with the changing weather than Colorado. Ellie found herself missing the colder temperature as she perused the general store, tailor, and supply depot, all the while looking for a thank you gift to take back to Molly, as the mayor trudged along beside her.

Otis visited the two young men in jail, and happened to find the sheriff in his office while he was there, giving him access to the arrest report, and the updated charge report. Jessie had been correct. The initial report was disorderly conduct for discharging a weapon within the town limit, as well as inside of an establishment. The original sentence was 72 hours in jail. However, 24 hours later, the charge was changed to murder for the deliberate killing of Samuel Harvey as an act of outlaw violence. He'd asked to see the witness statements, but the sheriff told him he wasn't privy to that information. He did give Otis a short list of names, whom he said were the witnesses. Surprisingly, the dice dealer's name was missing. The sheriff questioned who he was, since he'd been told the Doyle brother's attorney was J.D. Homer. Otis simply told him they were working together on the case, and left it at that.

After making a few notes, Otis left the sheriff's office and headed over to see Dr. Gordon, where he was shown the same coroner report that Jessie had viewed. Death by homicide was plainly written, and next to that was the detailed cause of blood loss due to multiple gunshot wounds. He asked a few questions about the body, then left for his final stop, the Cattleman's Saloon, where he found George Young, the dice dealer. The story Mr. Young gave him was exactly the same as the one Jessie had told him.

With all of his notes completed, Otis headed back to the hotel, arriving alongside Ellie and Mayor Montgomery, who'd finally completed their shopping excursion. Ellie carried a tuft of soft fabric and matching ribbon, wrapped up in brown paper with twine tied around it, forming a package.

"Did you find out anything?" Mayor Montgomery asked.

"A little more than the Lady Law," he replied. "I also met the sheriff."

"How did that go?"

"Fine until he started asking questions."

The three of them silenced themselves as they entered the hotel, each politely nodding to the desk clerk, before heading up the stairs.

*

Jessie was leaning against the window in her room when Ellie, Mayor Montgomery, and Otis walked in. She'd been expecting their arrival after having seen them walking on the street below.

"Well?" she asked, pushing off the wall and moving to stand near the tall dresser.

"What you have in your notes is correct. I saw the arrest report and updated charges. There really isn't a reason for the change. It goes from disorderly conduct for firing a weapon in the saloon, to murder for killing the man."

Jessie shook her head. "What about the sheriff?"

"He gave me a list of witnesses, but wouldn't let me see their statements. That's not uncommon, but it's usually a justifiable courtesy. Either way, George Young's name isn't on the list."

"So, he wasn't interviewed?"

"If he was, they're not using his statement."

"He was right in front of them and saw the entire argument," Jessie grumbled.

Otis nodded. "I know. I spoke with him. I also saw the coroner's report. Simply calling it a homicide leaves a lot of unanswered questions. I'm surprised with them changing the charges to murder, they didn't push for a more specific type of homicide."

"So, I was right. This is good?"

"It's something…but honestly, there isn't much here to go on. I'll present it to the justice in the morning, however, I wouldn't get my hopes up. They've built a strong case around very little to no evidence. If the sheriff is corrupt, as you say, then you don't know who else is with him. I've seen it before. These cases don't end well."

"What about the jury?" Jessie asked. "Do you know anything about them?"

"William and Billy waived their right, so it'll be a bench trial. It's also scheduled for first thing in the morning, and being held outside of the sheriff's office. They were setting up for it when I left."

"Are you serious?" Jessie growled.

"It sounded to me like they didn't know what it meant when they were asked if they wanted a jury trial. They both just said no."

Jessie shook her head. "Fred Clarence is using this to purposely get to me. He knows I'll be there. He is playing a dangerous game doing this out in the open."

"There has to be something we can do," Mayor Montgomery said. "Do you know anything about the justice?"

Otis shook his head. "I have no idea who he is."

Jessie balled her fist and brought it to her lips, lost in thought as anger and sadness boiled together inside of her.

Ellie wiped a tear from her own cheek. Knowing how hard this had to be for Jessie made her heart break.

Mayor Montgomery tapped Otis's shoulder and nodded towards the door when he noticed his trembles were returning. He kept the whiskey bottle in their room down the hall, but he'd also wanted to give Jessie some space to digest the severity of the situation. He only hoped she'd come to a rational decision.

"Please talk to me," Ellie said softly as the door closed, leaving her and Jessie alone in the room.

"There isn't much to say," Jessie sighed, plopping down on the edge of the bed. "He's going to kill my brothers, and he plans on me being here to watch him do it."

Ellie sat next to her and ran her hand over her wife's back.

"I found you because I traveled a long way to leave crooked men like him in my past. I—"

Ellie cut her off. "If you're going to say you're turning yourself in, I don't want to hear it. I can't bear losing you, Jessie."

92

"I was going to say I love you." Jessie's mouth formed a grin that quickly faded. "I honestly don't know what I'm going to do."

"I'll be by your side," Ellie said.

"No, you'll be with Mayor Montgomery. If something were to happen, I want you to be out of harm's way."

"Why must you always put yourself in the middle of the worst possible situations?"

"I don't plan on it. I believe that's just the way stars line up for me, unfortunately. You though, are a wrinkle in that line for sure. You're my true north." She smiled, kissing Ellie's lips softly as Ellie wrapped her arms around Jessie's neck.

FOURTEEN

Most of the town of Castor Valley was gathered around the end of Myer Alley, hoping to see the trial of William and Billy Doyle, which was being held outdoors on top of the raised platform, next to the sheriff's office. The large stage area was generally used for carrying out death by hanging sentences. A wooden podium was erected in the middle of the platform near the back edge, meant to be used as the justice's bench. Six chairs sat across the front of the platform in front of the podium. Three on one side and three on the other. Facing the podium from the street, Caldwell County Prosecutor, Jacob Smith, was in the first chair on the right. He had thick hair that looked almost bushy under his hat, and a full mustache and goatee. He was dressed in a dark suit and a ribbon bow-tie. To his right was Castor Valley Mayor, Benjamin Shaw. He had a large build that made him stand out a bit more than most men. He wore a dark suit with a blue paisley vest and a black neck tie. To the mayor's right sat Joe Clarence, the Castor Valley Sheriff. His hair was a mixture of white and the original reddish-orange color that had matched his brother's, and thick, bushy sideburns that didn't quite form muttonchops. He was dressed in a black suit with a black ascot tie. He sat with a menacing look on his face as his beady eyes scanned the crowd.

William and Billy were in the chairs on the opposite side of the podium, still wearing their dingy, soiled clothing. They both had light brown hair that was a few shades darker than Jessie's blonde hair, which was a trait she'd received from their father. Otis sat next to them, dressed in the same suit he'd arrived in, which was a size too big. However, the mayor had exchanged ties with him to make it look as though he'd changed his clothing.

Jessie stood in the back of the crowd, near the Hen House Diner, which was across the street. Mayor Montgomery and Ellie flanked her sides. She lowered the brim of her hat a little more than usual to escape eye contact with the sheriff, who seemed to be searching for her.

"I can't believe how many people are here, especially with tomorrow being Thanksgiving," Ellie mumbled.

"They don't care. They came to watch two men die," Jessie said in a low growl.

"Rise for the Honorable Justice, John Arthur White," the hangman announced from his position next to the platform.

The six men stood up from their chairs and turned their attention to the man who was walking up the side steps. He had thick, gray hair under a bowler hat, that was long enough to touch his collar, and a matching full beard. He wore a plain black suit with a wide, black neck-tie.

"You ever heard of him?" Mayor Montgomery asked.

Jessie shook her head. She hadn't been familiar with anyone on the right side of the law when she'd lived in Castor Valley.

"He looks like he's been at this a long time," Ellie sighed.

"Have a seat," Justice White said, stepping up behind the wooden podium, where he opened a leather note folder and read from the paper in front of him. "On this the 24th day of November in the year 1882, I, Justice John Arthur White, do hereby convene the murder trial of Castor Valley, Texas - Caldwell County, versus William John Doyle and

Billy John Doyle in the matter of the death of Samuel Robert Harvey. In the event of a guilty verdict, the sentence of death by hanging will commence immediately. A not-guilty verdict, will result in the direct release of the defendants." He turned the page and wrote a small note on the top of the next one. "This is a bench trial. There will be no jury present. I will listen to arguments from both the prosecution and defense, and make my decision based on the facts presented to me. Prosecutor, you may begin."

Jacob Smith stood up and walked to the center of the platform, facing the justice. "On the night of November 1st, William Doyle, Billy Doyle, and Samuel Harvey were involved in a game of dice inside the Cattleman's Saloon," he began. "An argument over the game resulted in all three men drawing pistols on each other. Samuel Harvey believed the defendants were cheating at the game. However, William and Billy Doyle, who are members of a vicious, murdering, thieving gang of outlaws who call themselves the Eldorado Gang, were using the game as a ploy in their plan to rob the saloon and all of the patrons."

"I object, your Honor. How can he know what their intentions were?" Otis interrupted.

"You'll get your turn," the justice said, nodding to the prosecutor to continue.

"As I was saying, the Doyle brothers, along with a woman, are wanted in several towns all over south Texas and across the border in Mexico. The men had been seen by witnesses, spending time in Castor Valley here and there over the course of several months, potentially forming the robbery they'd planned for November 1st. Yet, on this particular night, their plan was altered by the sudden argument between the defendants and Samuel Harvey, who subsequently brought negative attention to them by calling them out for cheating at the game. William Doyle and Billy Doyle drew their pistols first, pointing them at Samuel Harvey. Mr. Harvey drew his gun and fired three warning shots, purposely missing the two brothers. William and Billy then fired on Samuel Harvey, hitting him with two deadly bullets, causing him to die of blood loss almost immediately." Jacob Smith turned to the sheriff and mayor, before looking up at the justice and continuing.

Jessie wished she was closer. She could hear what he was saying, but it wasn't as clear as she'd have liked it to be, especially with whispers going on all around her. She strained her ears as he started talking once more.

"William Doyle and Billy Doyle were arrested in the saloon on November second, due to it being after the stroke of midnight, for disorderly conduct resulting in the death of Samuel Harvey. Later in the day, on November second, Sheriff Fred Clarence discovered the two men were connected to the Eldorado Gang and wanted in several counties, including Caldwell County. He began questioning witnesses and by those statements, he determined the real reason for the gang members to not only be in town, but also in the saloon. With this new information, Sheriff Clarence adjusted the charges from disorderly conduct to murder. Several town folk have alleged that the two brothers were very angry at Mr. Harvey for drawing attention to them, and shot him because he ruined their plan to rob the saloon."

Finished stating his case, the prosecutor sat down.

"Defense, you may proceed," the justice said.

Otis stood quickly and wobbled a bit before getting his bearings.

"Oh no," Ellie mumbled.

"You didn't give a him a drink, did you?" Jessie whispered.

"I couldn't send him up there puking everywhere," Mayor Montgomery whispered back. "I made sure he brushed his teeth three times, and he chewed on a couple of mint leaves."

Jessie sighed. Her brother's lives were in the hands of a drunken former attorney who despised her as he plead their case to a federal justice. *Could this get any worse?* she thought, trying to hear what Otis was saying.

"Whether or not William and Billy are or were members of an outlaw gang, has no purpose in this case," he started. "What happened on November first was unfortunate, but it was not murder. In fact, the coroner's report ruled it a homicide. Plain and simple. The fact is, William and Billy were playing dice in the saloon and were called cheaters by Samuel Harvey, after he'd lost to them. We all know that. The truth, however, based on witness statements, is Samuel Harvey was intoxicated, and he drew his gun first, firing four shots directly at William and Billy Doyle. None of these shots hit the men because Mr. Harvey was drunk. In order to keep him from actually shooting one of the brothers, or someone else in the saloon, William and Billy both shot Mr. Harvey in what they believed were places that wouldn't kill him, one in the upper arm and the other in the leg. Again, based on the coroner report and statement from Dr. Gordon, Samuel Harvey's wounds would not have killed him if the doctor had been summoned in a timely manner."

"Objection!" Jacob Smith argued.

"You had your turn. Let him speak," the justice said.

"William and Billy never once tried to leave the saloon after the shooting. In fact, they stayed to explain what had happened, and also asked why no one had gone for the doctor right away. The distance from the front of the saloon to the doctor's office is only a couple hundred paces at most." He paused to let the thought sink in.

"Let's go back to the shooting for a second. It's a known fact that at one time William Doyle and Billy Doyle were part of an outlaw gang. It's also a known fact that most outlaw gang members are good with a pistol. So, if these, as the prosecutor called them violent and angry, men were shooting to actually kill Mr. Harvey, why didn't they just shoot him in the head or chest? Why bother trying to give him a lesser injury? As vicious outlaws, they could've easily killed him, but they didn't. The truth is, they were only trying to stop him from hurting anyone. When a drunk man is firing a pistol all over the place, and you can't get close enough to grab him from behind, what would you do? They were good with guns and only had a second to think. The fact that Samuel Harvey died is not because the Doyle brothers shot him in self-defense. It's because the doctor wasn't summoned until it was too late."

*

"He certainly sounds like a lawyer," Ellie whispered.

"From what I heard, he was a pretty good one," Mayor Montgomery replied.

"What happened?"

The mayor shook his head.

Jessie kept her fists clenched at her sides. She wanted nothing more than to put a bullet through Fred Clarence's head just like she'd done to his horrible brother.

*

Otis looked at the two young men, then back at the justice. "Are William Doyle and Billy Doyle guilty of disorderly conduct resulting in the death of Samuel Harvey? You're damn right they are. They came into town without following the law and checking their guns. They were part of a scuffle that got out of hand. So, yes. That charge is correct. They've also served way more than the sentence of 72 hours locked up in jail. As for the charge of murder, there is no indication that a murder was committed. A homicide is simply death by another person, which was what was on the coroner's report, and also goes along with the charge of disorderly conduct resulting in death. A murder is planned. It's intentional. It's violent. What happened inside the Cattleman's Saloon wasn't planned. It wasn't intentional. And it wasn't violent. William and Billy Doyle didn't murder Samuel Harvey, but because Sheriff Clarence knew who they were…at one time in their lives, he changed the charges to murder in order to hang them for their past."

"You're wrong!" Sheriff Clarence yelled.

"Sheriff," the justice warned.

"They killed Samuel Harvey, and they deserve what's coming to them," the sheriff growled.

*

Ellie felt Jessie tighten next to her. "Don't," she whispered.

"I'm sorry," Jessie said to her, before yelling over the mass of people, "Fred Clarence, those boys didn't murder that man! You and I both know it! You're trying to settle an old score by doing this! Killing my brothers won't bring yours back! Let them go! I'm the one you have beef with! I'm Jessie Henry!" She removed her hat and tore the mustache from her face.

The crowd quickly parted, leaving a huge gap between the two of them.

Sheriff Clarence stood and drew his gun.

"No!" Ellie screamed.

Otis dove off the side of the stage like a coward.

"If you shoot me in cold blood, you'll hang!" Jessie yelled. "I'm a Town Marshal, and the mayor of that town is standing right here next to me!" she added. Her badge was clearly visible on her vest with the front of her jacket hanging open. "Now, you get your sorry ass down here and face me!"

"You're no law man! You're a woman!" the sheriff spat.

"No one says you have to be a man to be a marshal, at least not in our town," Mayor Montgomery yelled. "She's a sworn Town Marshal who has done more for our town than it looks like you've ever done for yours. Hanging two innocent men for something you *think* she may have done ten years ago, is about as corrupt and unjust as it gets. Don't you think, Mayor Shaw? What about you, Justice White?"

"Fred, what is all this? We don't need any trouble here," Mayor Shaw said.

"Trouble? She's an outlaw! A murderer!" he growled.

"I've never murdered anyone! Your no-good, piece of shit brother forced himself on me when I was just a kid! I got away before he could do it again! I won't deny I was an outlaw. I've never denied that, but those times are behind me. You show me proof of someone I actually murdered, and I'll tie that rope around my neck for you!" she yelled.

"All right! That's enough!" the justice shouted, smacking the wooden gavel on the top of the podium. "Sheriff, put that gun away before I have the hangman do it for you! I don't know what's going on here, but none of this nonsense pertains to this case."

"Actually, your Honor, it does. That woman down there is the sister to these two men. The sheriff of this town has been after her for several years for something she didn't do. He saw an opportunity to get her close by trying to hang her brothers. This is the reason for the murder charges. It was all a ploy to get to their sister," Otis stated. He was standing on the ground behind the platform.

The justice smacked the gavel on the podium again. "I'm ready to make my decision on this case," he said sternly.

"What about—" the prosecutor started and was cut off.

"I don't need to hear anymore," the justice barked.

Everyone stared at each other. The crowd was still silent from the argument between Jessie and Sheriff Clarence.

"In the matter of Castor Valley, Texas - Caldwell County, versus William John Doyle and Billy John Doyle for the murder of Samuel Robert Harvey, I find the defendants not guilty. However, I do find the defendants guilty of disorderly conduct resulting in the death of Samuel Harvey. They are both hereby sentenced to time already served in the Castor Valley jail. Gentlemen, you are both free to go."

Half of the crowd cheered, including Ellie, Jessie and Mayor Montgomery. The other half stood in shock, still reeling from everything that had transpired.

William and Billy jumped off the platform and hurried towards Jessie as fast as their malnourished, tired bodies could go. She ran too, wrapping her arms around them as they met.

"Mayor Shaw, I suggest you get a hold of whatever is going on in this town. Corruption is certainly not the way of the law, especially in the state of Texas," the justice added.

Mayor Shaw gritted his teeth. "I thought you said this was open and shut? I had no idea you were after someone else and using these innocent men to get what you wanted. Shame on you for wearing that badge."

"She killed my brother! She's a murderer! Why are you letting these outlaw murderers go?" the sheriff yelled. "If you won't stop them, I will!" he shouted, pulling his gun again.

"Jessie!" Ellie shrieked as Jessie dove on top of her, knocking her to the ground behind a water trough.

Mayor Shaw jumped off the platform with the justice as Sheriff Clarence began shooting. "Damn you, Fred Clarence! You're fired!" he yelled.

William and Billy took cover beside the nearby building, which was where Mayor Montgomery had gone. The people in the streets began running and screaming, unsure of where to go.

Still lying over Ellie as more shots rang out, Jessie drew her gun. She could see Fred's movements through a hole near the top of the trough.

"Come out you coward! I'm going to put you where you belong, and those hellions you call brothers are going with you!" Fred Clarence spat, scanning the crowd.

One of his deputies moved closer. "Come on, Fred. Drop the gun," he said gently.

Fred turned and fired one shot. The bullet struck the young man in the chest, and he fell off the back of the platform.

103

"Don't move," Jessie whispered into Ellie's ear as she adjusted her position.

She knew she only had one shot. Most of everyone around was unarmed, including her brothers and Mayor Montgomery, who were ten feet away. If she lifted her head, he'd see her movement and shoot in that direction. The pistol in her hand made a clicking sound as she pulled the hammer back with her thumb. She moved the pistol close to her chest, closed one eye to look through the hole, then stilled her breathing. In one quick motion, she popped her head and fired a shot. Fred's body ricocheted and crumbled to the ground with blood oozing from the hole in the center of his chest.

Jessie let out the breath she was holding and fell over onto her back, staring up at the blue sky above her.

Mayor Shaw and the justice climbed back up on the platform, checking Fred's body for signs of life. Neither knew who actually shot him since there was a no carry law in the town and the deputy had been killed.

"It's okay," Ellie whispered, leaning over and rubbing her hand over Jessie's cheek.

Jessie sat up and holstered her gun before moving to her feet.

"Is everyone okay?" Mayor Shaw asked.

Two bystanders had been hit by stray bullets, but they were both simple nicks in the arm.

"Is he dead?" one woman questioned as her husband pulled up from the ground.

"Yes," Mayor Shaw replied.

Mayor Montgomery walked over to Jessie and Ellie, with William and Billy following. Jessie stepped around them as Otis came running over.

"Come on, I need your help with one last thing," she said to him.

"I'm done," Otis huffed. "I nearly got killed up there!"

"Oh, for crying out loud, Otis. You dove off the platform before anything happened," she chided.

"That fee is getting a lot smaller," Mayor Montgomery said sternly.

"Fine," Otis grumbled. "Don't tell me you shot him," he added as they made their way back across the street, through the remaining people who were still getting up.

Jessie nodded.

"Wonderful…just wonderful," he muttered.

"You shot him?" Mayor Shaw asked, looking oddly at Jessie.

"Yes, sir," she said.

"Justice, you and I both know this was self-defense. Call it justifiable homicide if you want, but everyone saw that madman firing shots all over the crowd, purposely trying to hit her. I have at least thirty witnesses…" Otis stated.

The justice held his hand up to stop him from continuing.

"I see no reason to charge this woman. As far as I'm concerned, she saved all of our lives from a vindictive and corrupt man who was abusing his position of power. He murdered his deputy and attempted to murder several other innocent people. If anything, you'll be fined for carrying a gun in town. However, that's up to Mayor Shaw."

"No fine will be necessary," Mayor Shaw added. "So, you're the infamous Jessie Henry." He grinned and shook his head. "I've heard your name a time or two."

"About that, I was hoping we could get the local bounty removed," she replied.

"It's unjustifiable, especially after what was witnessed today," Otis added.

"I agree," the justice stated.

"Consider it done," Mayor Shaw said. "Now, if you're looking for a job…"

Jessie glanced over her shoulder at Mayor Montgomery and Ellie, who were across the street, more than likely talking about what had happened. She smiled. "No. I have one."

"As long as I am the Mayor of Castor Valley, the offer will stand."

She simply nodded. There was absolutely nothing that could make her want to stay in that town a minute longer.

"William and Billy," he added as they walked up. "I apologize for everything. You both went about things the wrong way, and so did Castor Valley."

The Doyle brothers nodded, and Otis walked away.

"If there are any fines assessed, I'll wire you the money. You can use it to pay for a new sheriff," Jessie said.

"We'll call it even," he replied.

Jessie and her brothers shook hands with the mayor and the justice before turning to walk away.

Ellie rushed across the street and into Jessie's arms. "I was scared to death," she murmured.

"Everything is alright."

"They're not going to charge you?" Ellie asked, leaning back to look into her eyes.

"No." Jessie shook her head.

"Oh, thank God!" she gasped, hugging her again. "I couldn't bear to lose you, Jessie."

"You're not going to. Not now…not ever." Jessie kissed her softly.

"Who are you?" Billy asked, clearing his throat as he watched the exchange between Jessie and Ellie.

"Boys, this is Ellie Henry...my wife," Jessie said, stepping aside to show off her beautiful companion.

"What?" they mumbled, looking at each other, then back at the two women.

"I'll explain everything later," Jessie replied, then she looked at Ellie and said, "I'll be there in a minute." She watched her walk away before turning back towards William and Billy.

*

"Surely, they're not coming back with us to Boone Creek," Otis muttered, noticing Jessie still talking with her brothers.

"She hasn't said," Ellie replied, hearing him as she walked up. "But, they are her family. They are welcome to come along."

"Great. More outlaws!" He huffed, taking a swig of whiskey from the hidden, glass drinking flask that he'd given him.

"Ease up on that. I'm not riding all the way home with a belligerent drunk," the mayor said.

"You just helped save her brother's lives and all you can say is they're all outlaws? Do you honestly have no compassion?" Ellie chided, shaking her head.

Otis lifted his chin and turned the other direction.

"For what it's worth, thank you for your help," she huffed. When Otis didn't answer, Ellie turned to Mayor Montgomery. "I'm sure they're as ready to get out of here as we are," she said, growing tired of the town folk staring at their small group.

"I booked the stage yesterday, so it's just waiting for us to show up with our bags," he said.

*

"I can't believe we're free," Billy muttered, shaking his head. "How did you figure all of this out? And who was that man you sent to help us?"

"He lives in the same town I live in, and I didn't bring him here. My wife and our town mayor did."

"He sure knew his stuff," William said. "I don't know how to thank you, Jessie."

"Come to Boone Creek with me. Start a new life…both of you," she said.

"Really?" Billy asked.

"Boys, I didn't leave because of you. I left because I was sick of that life. I wanted more. I'm sorry."

"Don't be. You tried to get us to stop," William sighed. "It actually took you leaving for us to see that we didn't want that life either."

"You know, we've been looking for you since the morning we woke up and you were gone," Billy added. "Are you really a sheriff?"

"No, I'm a town marshal. I live in a small town called Boone Creek, up in Colorado Territory. That man over there is Horace Montgomery. He's the mayor of Boone Creek, and a friend of mine."

"Do you think he'll let us come there?" Billy asked.

"Only if you're on the right side of the law. We have no place for outlaws, thugs, or any of the kind."

"We've been right since you left, Jessie. I promise. You know I wouldn't lie to you," William said.

"I know," she replied.

"Are there more women like your Ellie? She's so pretty and seems very nice," Billy said.

Jessie laughed. "I'm pretty sure she's one of a kind."

"I still can't believe you got married...and to a woman," William murmured.

"Did you ever see me with a man?" Jessie pinned him with a stare.

"Well, of course not. We knew you were with women. I just...I guess I never saw you as the settling down type, is all. I like her, though."

"Good, because she's everything to me. I think you'll both like her once you get to know her."

"Speaking of," Billy added, seeing Ellie heading towards them once again.

"I hate to interrupt, but Mayor Montgomery has a stage waiting. Don't you think it's about time we *all* started heading home?" Ellie said, smiling softly at Jessie.

Jessie wanted nothing more than to pull her wife into her arms and hold her at that moment. "Thank you," she whispered, meeting Ellie's eyes. "You heard her, let's get out of this hell hole," Jessie said.

"They're going to need tending to once we get into San Antonio," Ellie mumbled, walking alongside Jessie as they crossed the street.

Jessie laughed, knowing exactly what she meant. The odor wafting from William and Billy was downright horrid.

"Are we all set?" Mayor Montgomery asked.

"Yes," Jessie replied.

"Wonderful. I had our bags retrieved from the hotel. Gentlemen, do you have any belongings that we need to collect?" he asked the boys.

"No, Sir," they said together.

Jessie grabbed her satchel and removed the jar of hair and glue-paste. Then, she stepped aside and tossed them in a waste barrel. "I won't be needing those anymore." She grinned, handing the closed bag to the driver.

"I'm glad you finally got rid of that dreadful mustache," Ellie said, kissing her soft cheek.

"You don't want me to wear it at home?" Jessie teased.

"You won't have a home, if you do!" Ellie replied sternly.

Mayor Montgomery and Jessie's brothers laughed.

"You definitely had me fooled, especially with your long hair gone," Billy said.

"Did she have long hair when you met her?" William asked Ellie.

She shook her head.

"Jessie had hair past her shoulders. Looked like beautiful blades of yellow-white straw," Billy added.

"Really?" Mayor Montgomery questioned.

Jessie nodded. "I cut it off before I came to Boone Creek."

"She told me about it, but I would've loved to have seen it," Ellie said.

Jessie shook her head. "No mustache, no long hair."

Everyone laughed.

*

The stage driver strapped the bags to the roof and held the door open. Ellie climbed in first, taking the seat to the left. William and Billy went in next, sitting on the covered bench across from her. Mayor Montgomery got in after them, sitting on the same side as Ellie, but leaving a space in between them.

"I can't believe we're bringing them back with us," Otis muttered under his breath.

"If you want to ride up top with the bags, or perhaps run behind us, that can be arranged!" Jessie growled.

William and Billy glanced from one to the other as Otis squished in next to them.

"Is everything okay?" Billy asked.

"Everything's fine. His true colors are starting to come back. Otis is an ornery old cuss, you'll learn that soon enough, but he's all bark and no bite," Jessie reassured her brothers. She paused for a second, noticing a woman in the distance, who seemed to be headed their way. Shaking her head, she looked up at the driver. "Go on," she commanded. "Double time if you can," she added, climbing in and closing the door.

He slapped the reins, and the coach began to lurch down the road before Jessie could get situated, leaving the woman in the street behind them.

"Who was that?" Ellie whispered.

"My mother," Jessie stated.

FIFTEEN

During the half days ride back to San Antonio, Ellie fell asleep against Jessie's shoulder, still holding her hand; Otis drank himself to sleep; and Mayor Montgomery dozed off with his head against the side of the coach.

"I've robbed my share of these, but never actually rode in one," Billy said, referring to the luxurious stage.

"I felt the same way my first time. It was a pretty uncomfortable experience."

"They ride a lot smoother than a wagon or horse cart, that's for sure. How far are we going, anyway?"

"Across Texas and up through New Mexico, into Colorado. It'll take us about four days."

"By stage?" Billy questioned.

"No," Jessie laughed. "We'll be on a train for most of it."

"Never been on one of those either," he mumbled.

"My life is a lot different now. It took some getting used to, but I'd do it all over again."

"She must be something special," William added.

"Yes, but I changed my life for me. She's sort of an added bonus."

"Does she know we're not really your brothers?" William asked.

"No," she sighed. She'd been wondering when she should tell them, and with another couple of hours in their ride, now was as good a time as any. "No, because what I told her was the truth. I've never lied to her."

"What do you mean?" Billy questioned. "She called us your brothers. So did you, and that lawyer fellow did, too."

"That's because you are."

"What?"

Jessie wished she could maneuver herself to get to her jacket's inside pockets to light a cigar, but she was squished between Ellie and Mayor Montgomery. "I should've told you boys this a long time ago," she started. "Johnny Doyle is my father, too."

"What? How is that possible?" William challenged.

"My mother was a whore in Castor Valley. Johnny was one of her regulars…at least until she was with child."

"How do you know it was the same man?" Billy questioned.

"Because he came to town with both of you and your mother. Gertie called him out right in front of all of you, told him I was his. He refused to listen, and your mother refused to hear it. I never saw any of you again until the day you both walked into that saloon. I knew his name and about how old the two of you were, but that was it. It didn't take me long to put it all together."

William shook his, visibly angry with her.

"Why didn't you ever tell us?"

"I tried to get you to stay back and not follow me. Then, when you wouldn't take no for an answer, I had to protect you both. I knew if I'd told you, I never would've been able to leave the life I created for you. The life I wanted out of."

"So, you left us behind? Your own flesh and blood?" William snapped.

"William, I had no choice. You two were so caught up, you wouldn't listen when I talked about getting out. By that point, you were grown enough to know better."

"Our dad had light hair, almost as light as yours, and green eyes," Billy mumbled, actually noticing the resemblance for the first time.

"I know. Gertie always told me I looked just like him."

"I still can't believe this. Is this why you're here? Why you came to help us? Is it because you felt bad for leaving your own brothers behind?" William demanded.

"Yes and no. When I heard you were in trouble, I knew I had to go to you because you were my brothers. It wasn't because I left you behind. It was because I got you into that life in the first place. I've always resented that. It's why I tried so hard to get you out," she sighed. "It wasn't until I got here and figured out the truth, that I knew no matter what, I had to get you out."

"Did you think we murdered that guy?" Billy asked.

"No. Absolutely not. I know you've never murdered anyone. We've all killed people in self-defense, but none of us have ever purposely done it. Fred Clarence is the brother of Joe Clarence, the cattleman I'd worked with before running into the two of you. He forced himself on me. I got away from him, but he drew his gun. We fired at the same time. He missed, and I shot him between the eyes. I packed up and never looked back."

"It makes sense now," Billy said.

Jessie nodded. "William, I never meant to hurt either of you. Not in leaving like I did, and certainly not in telling you all of this. The two of you are my brothers, my own flesh and blood. I'd do anything for either of you."

"We were just kids back then, with no direction, no...no nothing. You came along and we clung to you, hanging on your every word," he muttered.

"I know, and I led you both down the wrong path. I had no idea where I was headed. Every road had come to an end

114

at that point, and there I was, contemplating how I was going to survive. I should've never brought you two along on that first robbery."

"Jessie, I don't fault you. You did what you had to do, and we did, too. Who knows where we would've ended up if we hadn't stayed with you," Billy said. "I've always thought of you as our big sister. I'm glad it's true."

"Thanks," she said with a smile, still looking at William, who was facing the window.

"William, you've said all along while we were looking for her, 'she's our family and we're going to find her'. We're all together again, and she really is our family. Let the past go. None of us can change it anyway," Billy said to his brother.

"I'm just…I guess I'm surprised. This whole situation has thrown me off a bit. You show up here, pretending to be a man that is our attorney. Then, another attorney shows up, saying he is working with you. Then, we find out we were charged with murder as bait because the sheriff has a beef with you from the past. Plus, you're a town marshal, carrying a badge, and you have a wife. Now, you're telling me you're our sister and we all share the same father." He shook his head. "I need a drink."

"I'm sure Otis has some whiskey," she said. "Billy, check his pockets for that drinking flask."

Billy searched around, careful not to wake the sleeping drunkard. He finally found the thin bottle and handed it to his brother.

"Go on. I'm sure the mayor has more to refill it with in his bag," she said.

William raised his brow.

"Otis is our town drunk. He's a grouchy, pain in the ass who hates me. On top of that, I don't think he's gone a day without being inebriated to some level, for several years at least. Trust me, you don't want to see him sober. Ellie said he began to sober up during their trip and started getting sick everywhere."

"Why does he hate you?" Billy asked.

"He thinks women can't be in law enforcement. I proved him wrong, then he found out I was an ex-outlaw. That only made it worse. Like I said, his mouth gets him into a lot of trouble, but he's harmless."

"Don't let her fool you," Otis mumbled, obviously having been woken up when Billy was looking for the flask. "She tried to drown me in a trough, and tried to shoot me more than once."

Billy chuckled.

"Otis, you can't pull that horse shit with these two. I taught them how to shoot. There's no *try*. If I'd wanted to shoot you, I would have," she chided.

"I have to agree with her," William said.

"More outlaws. Just what Boone Creek needs." Otis shook his head. "I'm sure you're going to be lawmen, just like her because being an outlaw gives you that privilege in our town."

"Otis, if you don't knock it off, I'm going to open the door and throw you out," Mayor Montgomery grumbled.

Jessie smiled.

"Actually, what *do* you plan to do when we arrive?" Mayor Montgomery asked, fully waking up.

"The only thing we've ever done is be outlaws and gamblers," William said. "But, we haven't done anything against the law in two years. We're right, now."

The mayor nodded. "Are they as good with a gun as you are?" he asked, looking at Jessie.

"I taught them everything they know."

"If that's the case, they might be able to fill those two deputy spots you've been asking for."

"I think that's a great idea."

"What is?" Ellie asked, stirring awake as the coach hit a jarring bump.

"William and Billy becoming deputies," Jessie replied, running her thumb over the back of Ellie's hand.

"Is that what you both want to do?"

"Sure," William said.

"Why not?" Billy shrugged. "We're good with guns and tracking outlaws. We made a lot of money on bounties when we were all together, didn't we, Jessie?"

She nodded.

Ellie pursed her lips in thought. "What do you think Bert is going to say about all of this?"

"He's going to be upset with me. I didn't tell him exactly what was going on. I only said I was going to help with a family matter."

"I did the same thing with Molly. I'm sure they will understand."

"Who is Bert?" William asked.

"He's my deputy, and my friend. He's been at my side since I became the town marshal. We've been through a lot together. He's been like my right hand."

"Do you think he'll be okay working with us?" Billy questioned.

"Yes. Will the two of you be okay working on the right side of the law, and with someone else in our group, who outranks you?" she asked pointedly as the stage came to a stop.

William and Billy both said, "Yes."

"Where did you get the name J.D. Homer? I thought maybe it was someone you knew or something," Billy questioned.

"I was wondering the same thing," Ellie added.

"It's a little simpler than that. J.D. is from Jessie and Diabla, and Homer was my first horse. Well, he wasn't exactly *mine*. He was a medium-sized, grey gelding, with a short, black mane. He was used by the town, mostly for stages. I took care of him at the stable and livery. That's where I spent the majority of my childhood. Anything was better than hanging around the whorehouse, where I was banished to my room in the attic. Anyway, I'd never been on a horse. After taking care of Homer for some time, the stable manager let me take him for a ride. I was scared out of my mind. He felt how tense I was and bucked, nearly throwing me to the ground, but I held on tight. He stood in the street, with me up in the saddle, not moving at all. As soon as I calmed down and eased up on the reins again, he trotted off slowly. It wasn't long before I was riding that horse all over town. He trusted me and I trusted him."

"What happened to Homer?" Ellie asked.

"If I could've taken him with me, I certainly would have, but he was already older when I first met him. I'm sure he died not long after I left."

"Your time together probably extended his life," Ellie said.

Jessie nodded in agreement. "We're here," Jessie stated as the coach trotted down Middle Street in San Antonio, headed towards the stage office.

*

After a quick trip to the barber, and then the bathhouse, William and Billy were looking and feeling more like themselves again. Jessie had gone to the tailor and purchased a new suit and hat for each of them, which Mayor Montgomery delivered to them in the bathhouse.

When they stepped outside, Jessie was blown away. She was finally looking at her brothers again, but she'd also never seen them dressed in anything other than the dingy frontier clothes they'd all worn back when they were outlawing together. Both men had neatly trimmed hair, combed with wax, and their scraggly beards were replaced with clean-shaven faces. Although Billy had opted to keep his thick, sandy-brown mustache, he still had a boyish appearance.

Ellie noticed the subtle resemblance in the siblings when they all stood together, smoking cigars. Albeit, Jessie was the only one with blonde hair and green eyes. The boys had sandy brown hair and brown eyes, more than likely traits from their mother.

"I've never felt so...I don't know. Odd, maybe?" William said, looking down at himself in the new attire.

"I like it. I think it makes me refined," Billy said, spinning around to get the full effect. "What do you think, Jessie?"

"I think you both look like the men I know you've grown up to be," she replied, then added, "Come on, the train leaves in a few minutes. Mayor Montgomery was able to book us a sleeping coach."

"I've never been on a train," Billy mumbled, taking it all in as they walked towards the rail station. He could see the locomotive of the train, jutting out past the ticket office. White smoke billowed from the stack.

"Me either," William added.

119

"Well, you're going to ride on two of them, because otherwise, it'll take you a month to get to Boone Creek," Jessie stated, stepping between them and placing her hands on their backs.

*

The train was barely an hour outside of El Paso, when everyone, but Jessie, was fast asleep. The sleeping coach had double, fold down bunks, one over the other, along both sides, with an aisle up the middle. Mayor Montgomery was at one end, above Otis, with William and Billy at the other end, across from each other up top. Ellie and Jessie were towards the middle of the coach, with Jessie on the upper bunk.

Jessie stared out the window at the stars as the darkness passed by. The moon casted shadows on the desert rock formations in the distance. This was her third time taking the long journey through the plains of West Texas; she silently hoped it would be her last. With her brothers accompanying her home to Boone Creek, the only thing she'd left behind was memories of a place and time she'd hoped to one day forget. There was nothing left in Castor Valley for her to ever go back to, that she was sure of.

*

When the train lurched to a stop at the El Paso station, the sun was slowly beginning to paint the sky orange with beautiful hues of red and yellow mixed in. Jessie finished her cup of coffee and grabbed her bag.

As soon as they disembarked, the group headed to the ticket window to inquire about their next train, which would take them north, through New Mexico Territory, and into Colorado Territory. Mayor Montgomery paid for tickets for himself and Otis, while Jessie paid for everyone else, a feat that nearly wiped out the remainder of the money she'd taken with her. She checked the coin purse that was stored inside the interior pocket of her jacket. She always kept a handful of coins in her vest pocket, of varying amounts. However, she'd taken her coin purse on the trip, so she'd be able to easily carry more money. Looking at the three golden eagles, and couple of trade dollar coins, she sighed and cinched the bag. She'd spent way more than she'd ever planned, but she'd still had a little more than enough to secure passage for herself, Ellie, and her brothers, in the stagecoach once they reached Red Rock.

"I'll be along in a minute," Jessie said as the group began to head over to the next train, which was scheduled to leave within the half hour.

Ellie watched her curiously as she turned down a side street.

"Where's she going?" Billy asked.

"Hopefully, to get more whiskey," Otis mumbled.

Ellie pinned him with a stare, but refused to let him bother her.

"She said something about posting Bert. I'm sure he's about lost his mind by now," Mayor Montgomery said.

"Bert? The deputy?" William questioned.

"Yes. He and his wife, Molly, are friends of ours. In fact, she's keeping shop for me in my store right now. They're good people."

"Boone Creek has a lot of nice and decent town folk. Especially now, since Jessie ran all of the outlaws off," the mayor added. "We do have our fair share of troublemakers from time to time." He looked over at Otis. "But, Jessie does a great job of maintaining law and order in our town."

"We might as well board," Ellie said. "She'll be along in a minute."

"After you," Mayor Montgomery replied, tipping his hat to her.

Ellie glanced back one last time, before moving past him and stepping onto the platform.

*

Steam from the locomotive rose in the air as the boiler heated. The whistle blew one last time, indicating their departure as Jessie slid into her seat next to Ellie, squeezing her hand.

"Everything okay?" Ellie asked, looking into the green eyes that always tugged at her heart.

"Yes. I sent a post to Bert. There were more people in their than I'd expected," Jessie sighed. "I had to wait in line," she added, looking around the train coach.

They were in first class, just as they had been on the last train. However, this coach was currently set up as a passenger coach, with back to back seats. During overnight trips, the seats would flatten, and the overhead bins would fold down, converting it to a sleeper coach. Their scheduled arrival in Red Rock was early evening, so they'd be completing the rest of their train journey with the seats in their current position.

Luckily, they were all able to sit together in two side by side sections with Mayor Montgomery and Otis beside Ellie and Jessie, on the opposite side of the aisle, and her brothers were in the backwards seats across from them.

Jessie noticed William peering through the window at the mountain ranges on both sides of the train, one of which ran along the Rio Grande. The train coach made a clicking sound, lulling from side to side, as it was pulled along the tracks. "It's beautiful out here, isn't it?" she muttered.

He nodded in agreement.

"How much longer do we have to travel?" Billy asked, running his hand along the velvet-covered bench cushion he was sitting on.

"We should get into Red Rock this evening. If we can get a group stage, we'll be home by tomorrow night. They're much faster with the additional horses," she answered.

"I posted ahead with our request. Hopefully, they'll get it in time," the mayor added.

SIXTEEN

The final leg of their journey was a bumpy, stagecoach ride from Red Rock to Boone Creek. Jessie had felt the cold chill in the air as soon as they'd exited the train, but she hadn't noticed the snow on the ground until they were well underway.

"Everything looks so beautiful when it's covered in white snow," Ellie said, thankful she'd thought to bring her shawl as she wrapped it a little tighter.

"Yeah," Jessie agreed. "Christmas will be here soon," she added. Last year, they'd shared the holiday with Bert and Molly. She silently wondered what the day would look like now that her brothers would be in town.

"I don't suppose you'll find me a duck this year," Ellie said.

"A duck?" Jessie raised a brow. "I thought it's supposed to be a turkey?"

"That's Thanksgiving," Ellie answered. "Anyway, I happened to like duck better."

Jessie nodded.

"There aren't any ducks in Colorado. At least not this time of year," Mayor Montgomery stated.

"I guess there's always mouse." Ellie grinned, trying to keep a straight face.

"Don't plan on Bert helping you out with that one." Jessie shook her head.

"Mouse?" Mayor Montgomery grimaced.

"It's a long story," Jessie sighed.

"Desert rat isn't bad, right Jessie?" Billy said.

"That's true," she agreed.

"You ate a rat?" Ellie muttered, skewing her face in disgust.

"Times were hard. We did what he had to do," Jessie replied.

"Rattlesnake was pretty good. Although, catching them wasn't all that fun," William added.

"Well, we definitely do not have rattlesnake or rat on the menu at the Kettle Kitchen," Mayor Montgomery stated. "They do serve some pretty good pork and beef dishes, though."

"That's fine with me." Billy smiled.

Jessie glanced at Otis, who was passed out, and shook her head. Hearing the way he'd spoken to the justice back in Castor Valley, definitely sounded like he knew what he was doing at some point in his life, at least. The stage hit a rut that caused the coach to bounce. Otis opened his eyes, but not before Jessie turned her attention back to the window.

It was the middle of the day, so the bright sun glistened against the inch or so of crisp, white snow in the distance. Albeit, Jessie was sure the trail they were riding along was covered in mud.

*

"Brrrr," Billy mumbled as his teeth chattered. He squished his arms in and rubbed his hands together, trying to stay warm. The coach had finally arrived in Boone Creek, just after dark. The streets were lit by kerosene lamps that cast the small town in a yellowish glow. A light dusting of snow covered everything.

"It's definitely colder here than it is in Texas, boys," Jessie said, noticing how cold both of her brothers were.

"Is this as bad as it gets?" Billy asked, slightly shivering.

"I'm afraid it gets much colder, and thick blankets of snow cover everything in sight, turning the streets to muddy mush," Jessie replied, turning back towards the stage to help retrieve the bags.

Otis had pretty much walked away without saying a word after Mayor Montgomery handed him a handful of gold coins. The mayor shook his head and sighed.

"I understand why you brought him, and I'm grateful he was able to help, but I doubt he's going to change his ways," Jessie muttered.

"Oh, I'm sure he won't. Hell, he's already gone back to hating you," he laughed.

She simply shrugged. "I don't know how to thank you…for everything. You didn't have to come all that way and help me, especially after I wasn't completely honest with you." The mayor went to speak, but Jessie held up her hand. "Let me finish. I know Ellie is stubborn as a day is long, so thank you for making sure she was safe. I'm sure she was determined to go, whether you wanted to or not. Whatever you spent on travel, Otis, and anything else, take it out of my pay. That's the least I can do," she finished, holding her hand out.

He shook her hand, then pulled her in for a half hug. "You can thank me by continuing to keep this town, and the people who call it home, safe."

Jessie nodded.

"You and Ellie, you're like family to me. I'd do it all over again…but don't get anymore wild ideas about leaving town." He grinned.

Jessie laughed.

"Take a day or so to get settled, then bring your brothers by my office. We'll get them sworn in," he said, turning to walk away.

"I thought you needed to check the budget?" Jessie called.

"I'll make it work," he replied over his shoulder.

Jessie looked around the docile street, feeling a huge weight lift off her shoulders. It was nice to be *home*. "Come on, boys, before you freeze to death," she said, wrapping her arm around Ellie to help keep her warm as they walked down Main Street towards the General Trade.

William and Billy trudged along behind them, too cold to look around at the town.

*

"I know it's not much, but—" Ellie started, moving around the room with a walking candle while Jessie lit the stove to heat the room they called home.

"It's perfect," Billy replied.

"Anything is better than the filth in that jail," William added. "Thank you."

"William and Billy, you two can have the chairs in front of the stove. That'll keep you warm all night. We'll figure out a better solution in the morning," Jessie said, stoking the fire one last time before walking over to the nearby area where her and Ellie's bed was located. She moved the dressing curtain, forming a slight partition between the two areas to give them some form of privacy.

William and Billy stripped down to their suit pants and shirts, which they kept over their underclothes. Ellie had provided each of them with a thin blanket, which they'd gladly accepted.

Jessie made sure they were comfortable one last time, then walked around to her bed. She stripped down to her underclothes and pulled the quilt back before climbing into bed.

Ellie slid over and into her open arms. She couldn't shake the sense of relief she felt being back home in her own bed with Jessie. "I love you," she whispered.

"I love you, too," Jessie murmured, softly kissing the top of her head.

*

The next morning, Jessie awoke to an empty bed. She quickly pulled her pants and shirt on before peering around the makeshift partition. William and Billy were just waking up. She finished dressing, then walked over to them.

"Morning." She smiled, still getting used to seeing them. The past two weeks had felt somewhat like a bad dream. "When you're ready, head downstairs and walk across the street to the Marshal's Office. I have some business to take care of, but after that, we'll go over to the Kettle Kitchen and get some breakfast. Then, I'll show you around town," she added, pouring herself a cup of coffee from the pot on the stove.

"Sounds good to me," Billy mumbled sleepily.

William nodded, looking around the kitchen area.

"Cups are in that cabinet by the sink," she said, before heading down the spiral staircase.

*

Ellie stood near the register counter, talking with a customer, when Jessie made her appearance.

"Good morning, Marshal," the townsman said, tipping his hat as he grabbed his purchase and headed towards the door.

"Did I scare him off?" Jessie questioned.

"No." Ellie grinned. "He'd already paid for his purchase, and was inquiring about where I'd been. It seems Molly couldn't tell him when my cinnamon apple cider would be ready."

"Oh." Jessie nodded. "And when might that be?"

"Well, it was supposed to be a few days ago, but...since I had to go traipsing all over creation recently, it'll be next week," she replied as her lips formed that 'don't mess with me' smile that her wife was very familiar with.

Jessie stepped closer, careful not to touch Ellie as she leaned in, whispering, "You traipse pretty well."

Ellie laughed and pushed her away.

"You've returned!" Molly called, stepping inside and quickly hugging her friends.

"Good to see you," Jessie said. "I should probably get over and let Bert know I'm back. The boys will be down in a minute. I'm going to take them for breakfast and show them around."

"Good idea. We need to work on our situation," Ellie replied, pulling her eyes up to the ceiling. "They snore louder than a train whistle."

Jessie chuckled. "I'll figure something out."

Ellie watched her leave, before turning back to Molly.

"How did your trip go?" Molly asked.

"In short...Jessie nearly got herself hung by a crooked sheriff. She and Otis just about scratched each other's eyes out. Oh, and her brother's are upstairs. We brought them back with us."

"My word!" Molly gasped, putting her hand over her mouth to hide her grin. "A least you *all* made it back safely. I presume."

"Yes." Ellie nodded. "We got in late last night. Thank you so much for watching the store. I'll cut you in on the earnings for the week."

"There's no need to do that." Molly shook her head. "That's what friends do. They help each other in times of need. Besides, the knitting ladies from church just adore Eddie."

"I was wondering where he was."

"I dropped him off on my way here. I know Jessie posted Bert, saying you'd be back today, but I wasn't sure what time. So, I was prepared to open the store." She smiled. "It seems you beat me to it."

"I was up earlier than usual," Ellie sighed. "Speaking of," she added, hearing the boys coming down the stairs.

"Molly, this is William Doyle and Billy Doyle, Jessie's younger brothers. This is Molly Boleyn, Bert's wife. He's the Deputy Marshal."

"Nice to meet you, Ma'am," they said politely. "Jessie told us to meet her at her office," Billy added.

"Across the street," Molly answered.

William and Billy said goodbye before donning their hats and heading out of the store.

"They look like Jessie," Molly said, watching them walk away.

"Yeah," Ellie agreed. "They all share the same father, but Jessie had a different mother. She's the oldest by about three years, I think."

"It's been a while since we had nice looking, single, young men around town. Miss Mable ought to be happy."

"Ugh, don't get me started on that place."

Molly laughed, knowing how all of the women in town hated brothel.

SEVENTEEN

"I hope you cleaned the horse shit off those boots," Jessie mumbled, peering through the open doorway of the Marshal's Office at Bert. He was sitting at her desk with his feet propped up on the corner, similar to the way she sat when reading the newspaper.

"I haven't stepped in horse droppings…at least, not recently," he said, dropping his feet to the floor and standing up. "Welcome home." He smiled, holding his hand out.

"Thanks. How was everything around here?" she replied, shaking his hand.

"Fine. Same stuff we usually deal with: drunken brawls and travelers carrying firearms. Nothing I couldn't handle."

"Where is your desk?" she asked, looking around.

"The leg broke. It's over getting repaired," he replied. "How was your trip?"

"Eventful," she muttered.

"I figured you might have run into trouble when the mayor and Ellie left town a week later. Is everything okay now?

"Sit back down," she said, nodding towards her desk chair. Bert looked oddly at her, but did as instructed. "I have two younger brothers. They were outlaws with me in the gang I led," she paused, watching his face. "When I left, they went right and spent the last two years trying to find me, mostly hanging around my home town, hoping I'd return someday. They got caught up in a mess, which led

132

them to a crooked sheriff who was out for blood…my blood, to be exact."

"What? Why?"

"I killed his brother," she stated.

Bert stiffened and the whites of his eyes grew slightly larger.

"It was self defense, and it's a rather long story," she sighed. After going through the memories of her time with Joe, over and over in the last few weeks, she hoped she never had to visit them again. "Anyway, his brother is now the sheriff in the town that I'm from. He falsely claimed my brothers murdered a man whom they got into a confrontation with, all as a corrupt ploy to get to me. Obviously, it worked. I ran straight to them."

"Oh, my word. Who would do such a thing?"

"Someone driven by vengeance," she muttered.

"Don't tell me he hung your brothers."

"No…Ellie and Mayor Montgomery arrived with Otis, who apparently is an ex-Texas lawyer. He defended them to the justice, then things got a bit crazy when the sheriff tried to shoot me in front of the entire town."

"What? Wait…Otis? As in drunk Otis?"

Jessie nodded. "Took me by surprise, too. He was pissed, but the mayor threatened to toss him off the train on the way home if he didn't help me."

Bert laughed. "I'm sorry, I know it was serious, but I still can't picture Otis talking to a justice. Was he sober?"

"Hell no. Every time he got close to it, he became sick and ornery. Mayor Montgomery kept him slightly inebriated the entire time."

Bert shook his head in disbelief. "So, what happened with the crooked sheriff?"

"I told him who I was and called him out on the corruption. That's when he pulled his gun. Fortunately, the justice saw the entire thing, and based on the evidence against my brothers, they hadn't intended on killing the man. They were set free and the justice had the sheriff locked up."

"You always seem to find trouble." Bert smiled, shaking his head. "What about your brothers? Where are they now?"

"That's what I wanted to talk to you about. They're here, actually."

"Really?"

"Yes. They should be here any minute."

Bert leaned forward and glanced out the door to the empty street.

"Mayor Montgomery finally came through on my request for more deputies," she said.

'That's good," he replied, turning his attention back to her.

"He hired my brothers."

"Oh," he mumbled, nodding slightly.

"They've never been in law enforcement, but their cut from the same cloth I am. They'll be a good fit, but it'll take some getting used to…for us, and for them."

"I see."

"I apologize for not telling you exactly why I had to leave," she said.

"What you went through couldn't have been easy. I wish you and Ellie would've told us the full truth. We would've stepped up to help you both out anyway. That's what friends are for."

"I know." Jessie nodded. "Even after two years, the ghosts of my past are still shadowing me. I didn't want to get anyone else involved. If I had known Ellie was coming, much less bringing the Mayor and Otis with her, I would've never posted her. However, I'm glad things happened the way they did. I cut the rest of my ghosts loose, and left them behind. And, now I have my brothers back in my life." Hearing a noise outside, Jessie turned towards the door. "Speaking of them, here they come," she said.

Bert watched as two men stepped inside. They were dressed in dark suits, with different ties, but still similar to Bert and Jessie. He noticed the resemblance as soon as he looked at the three of them standing together.

"Morning, boys. This is my deputy and my friend, Bert Boleyn. This is William Doyle and Billy Doyle, my brothers."

"Welcome to Boone Creek. It's nice to meet you," Bert said, standing to shake hands with each of them. "Jessie tells me you'll both be joining us."

"I believe so," William replied.

"We just met your wife over at the trade store," Billy said.

"Molly." Bert smiled.

"I need to get them over to the mayor's office to make everything official. Then, I'm going to show them around. I have a few others things to do, but I'll check back in with you in a little while," Jessie said.

Bert nodded as he watched them scurry off with Jessie pointing out various buildings in town.

*

"Here is the church," Jessie said. "Pastor Noah has a keen sense of people. He's nothing like any preacher man I've ever met."

"You go to church?" William stammered, slightly shocked.

"No. I've never set foot in there. The damn place would probably burn to the ground," she stated. "He comes outside and talks with me from time to time. He also leaves a stool out for me to sit on and listen to his sermon once a month."

William raised a brow, giving her an odd expression.

"It's a deal we have. That's as close as I'll get, and he knows it. Ellie goes every Sunday. She even sits up front."

Billy chuckled lightly.

"Well, if it isn't our lovely Town Marshal," Pastor Noah said, noticing her passing by the open doorway. "Who do you have here?"

"Pastor, these are my brothers, William and Billy."

"My word," he said with a smile. "Welcome to Boone Creek. Are you two planning on staying in our charming little town? Or are you passing through?"

"Actually, they've moved here," Jessie replied.

"Yes, we're going to be deputies," Billy added.

"Is that so?" Pastor Noah questioned.

"Yes, sir," William answered.

"Are you as good as this woman right here?" the pastor asked. "She just about single-handedly cleaned up this town, with Bert's help of course." He smiled.

"She taught us everything we know." Billy grinned.

"Well, it sounds like you're good to go then. You gentlemen should come to one of my sermons. I hold them every Sunday morning."

"Oh, I don't believe we'll be doing that, but thank you for the offer," William replied.

"They really are your brothers." Pastor Noah shook his head and laughed. "I promise you won't go up in flames.

Everyone is invited to hear God's word. He doesn't judge the living. The sins of thou soul pay penance long after thy body has left this world."

"That's good to know," William mumbled.

"I'll leave a couple of extra stools outside. We'll start there," the pastor said, before they continued on.

"He's certainly different," Billy muttered.

"Yes, he is. He married Ellie and I, and for that, I will be forever grateful."

"Is that why you sit outside on the stool and listen to him preach?" Billy asked.

Jessie nodded. "That was part of our deal. Anyway, here's the mayor's office," she said, pointing out the two story building. "The first level is his home, and his office is upstairs."

William and Billy followed her as Jessie opened the door and walked inside, removing her hat. The foyer had a wall to the left, a locked door to the right, which was the entrance to his private quarters, and a grand staircase straight ahead that led up to his large office.

"Good morning, Marshal...gentlemen. Have a seat," he said. "Cigar, anyone?"

They each took a cheroot from the box, grabbed a match from the holder on the mayor's desk, and lit it. White, sweet-scented, smoke curled around the room.

"I assume you are both still interested in working for the town of Boone Creek as Deputy Marshals."

"Yes, sir," William and Billy replied.

"Wonderful. I'm sure Marshal Henry is ready to put you both to work." He smiled. "We do have a few formalities to discuss. First of all, have you worked out your living arrangements? Miss Mable only has one border room available, I believe. There are a couple of rental houses that are open, and the hotel also has border rooms, but they come at a much higher price than Miss Mable's place."

"We have that taken care of," Jessie added.

"We do?" Billy asked.

Jessie nodded.

William furrowed his brow. "We can't all live in that one room."

"We won't be," she said. "Go on, Mayor."

"All right." He moved on, discussing their pay and job description, and both men agreed with his terms. Then, he added a stipulation about following Territory Law, which made him glance at Jessie. As good as she was at being the Town Marshal, even after two years, she still reverted back to Frontier Law from time to time. Mayor Montgomery was sure this was why his graying hair had turned nearly all white.

Jessie bit back a grin as she puffed on her cigar.

"That brings me to the final point. I'll leave it to Marshal Henry to handle training, and the hierarchy within the Marshal's Office. Understand that I may give my opinion, but I stand behind each and every decision that she makes in that regard. She is highly respected in this town, and by this office. Now, if you'll both stand, we'll get you sworn in, so you can get to work."

Jessie stood aside, watching as her brother's took the oath, one at a time. Mayor Montgomery pinned badges onto their vests, and shook their hands. Then, he added their names, vital information, and their gun types into the record log, making everything official on paper.

"They're all yours," he said to her.

"Wonderful. Thank you again, Mayor…for everything," she replied, shaking his hand.

"No need to thank me. Just keep this town and the people who call it home…safe. That's all I ask of you."

"You have my word," she replied. "Come on, deputies. Let's go get you settled in."

"Jessie, one last thing," he called, handing her a skeleton-style key. Then, he slid two identical pieces of paper across the desk. She read over them, then signed both. "It's all yours."

"Wonderful." She smiled, walking away to meet her brothers in the hallway.

EIGHTEEN

Jessie led William and Billy around Main Street Curve and back towards Center Street. Many of the town folk tipped their hats and said hello to the trio as they passed by.

"This seems so surreal," Billy said. "All three of us walking down a street with law badges pinned to our chests."

"Yeah, it took me a while to get used to it," Jessie uttered.

"Never thought I'd see this day," William added. "So, what's it like around here? Is there a lot of trouble? The people seem nice."

"They are. We have the exceptional few who like to start trouble, but I've run off the major outlaws. This place was starting to look like Tombstone when I arrived, everyone running amuck. The former Marshal allowed it, and the town folk simply lived with it because they were all scared. I changed that."

"I was going to ask how you wound up with a badge," William said.

"I rode into town on a half-dead horse, so this was as far as I was going. Anyway, I arrived and no sooner than I tied the horse's reins, did I hear yelling in the street behind me. I turned in time to see two outlaws shoot and kill the marshal, who hadn't even drawn his gun. Out of instinct, I drew and shot them both, right off their horses. Then, I walked into the saloon to spend the last couple of coins I had left in my pocket, drowning myself in cheap, rotgut whiskey before begging for a job as a game dealer. Mayor

Montgomery walked in and offered me the job since he was in need of a town marshal, and I seemed like I knew what I was doing."

"Are you serious?" Billy questioned, slightly stunned.

"Absolutely," she replied with a nod.

"Did he know you were an outlaw?" William asked.

"I didn't say it, but I was sure he suspected it. The whole town knows about my past...now, anyway. It's not a secret," she sighed, thinking about the trouble that had gone down a little over a year ago. "Everyone...well, mostly everyone, accepts me for who I am now, not what I did back then. I've cleaned up the town, with Bert's help of course. Together, we've made it a safe place to live. It's become my home. The only home I've ever really had."

"You do seem a lot different," Billy said.

"I am in some ways, but I'm still the same Jessie Henry in a lot of ways, too," she replied, turning a corner. "Boys, this here is Six Gun Alley. If there's going to be trouble in Boone Creek, this is where it will be. That over there to the right is the back door to the Rustler's Den Saloon. Next to it is the bath house. To our left, and adjacent to the saloon, is Miss Mable's brothel house. The rest of the buildings are rental houses, all of which are full. At the very end, back towards the entrance to the town, is Doc Vernon's office. He lives in the room on the second floor."

"Marshal Henry, I haven't seen you around much lately," Lita called from her position on the upstairs balcony in the brothel.

"I was traveling."

"No doubt with that wife of yours. Rumor was she was gone, too."

"That's correct."

Lita shook her head and pushed her bosom out further as she leaned forward, nearly causing her breasts to spill over the top of her red and black corset. "Who are these fine gentlemen?" she asked with a smile, eyeing the boys up and down.

"Not interested," Jessie stated. "Come on, I might as well introduce you to Miss Mable," she said to her brothers. "She was kind enough to let me border a room, on the town's expense of course. She's quite nice. Ellie doesn't think much of her, or this place, for that matter. Neither does Bert. But, when I'm making my rounds through town, I always stop and check on Miss Mable."

"What about that one up on the balcony?" Billy asked, glancing up at Lita.

"She's a handful."

"How so?" he asked.

"She wanted me as a companion, and I wasn't interested, which I'd made rather clear. When Ellie and I began courting, she tried to cause trouble."

"Oh," he mumbled, walking in behind Jessie as they entered the house.

"Take your hats off," she hissed, removing her own.

"Well, Marshal Henry," Miss Mable drawled. "What brings you by on this lovely morning?" she asked, batting her eyes at the boys.

"I'd like to introduce you to our newest Deputy Marshal's, William Doyle and Billy Doyle. You'll be seeing them from time to time. I wanted you to know who they were."

"Wonderful. Both named Doyle…are you brothers?"

"Yes, ma'am." Billy smiled. "And Jessie is our sister."

"Is that so?" Miss Mable's face wrinkled with surprise. Jessie nodded.

A few of the painted ladies made their way into the parlor where Jessie, her brothers, and Miss Mable were located.

"Girls, these men are our newest Deputy Marshal's, and they're Marshal Henry's brothers," she cooed.

"It's nice to meet you, ladies," the brothers said, with Billy adding a boyish smile.

"Charming and handsome," Lita remarked, making her way down the stairs. "Where have you been hiding these two, Marshal?"

"We were back home in Texas," Billy answered.

"And were you outlaws, too?" she asked, moving closer to him.

"Now, Lita…" Miss Mable chided.

"They ran with me, yes," Jessie replied. "All of that is in the past, and I'd like to keep it there."

"Understood," Miss Mable said, giving Lita a stern look.

"We won't keep you. I simply wanted to introduce them around town today."

Miss Mable nodded. "Did either of you happen to need a room? I believe we have one border available."

"Actually—" William started.

"No. They have a place," Jessie said, cutting him off as they headed out the door.

"Well, if anything changes, the offer stands. And gentlemen, feel free to come by anytime. Our door is always open."

Jessie put her hat back on and ushered them across the street.

"We can't stay with you and Ellie forever," Billy said.

"I know. Just trust me," she replied, entering the saloon.

"Marshal Henry!" Elmer called. "How was your trip?"

"Eventful to say the least," she sighed as she sat on a stool. Her brothers flanked her sides as they sat down. She held up three fingers, and Elmer went to work, pouring three thimbles of whiskey.

"Isn't it a little early for you?" Elmer asked, setting the cups down.

"We just left Miss Mable's," she muttered.

Elmer laughed. "In that case, would you like the bottle?"

Jessie grinned. "Elmer, meet our two newest Deputy Marshals and my brothers, William and Billy Doyle," she said as he slid the cups over to the trio. "Boys, this is Elmer. He's the owner of this place…and a friend."

"Oh my," he gasped, wiping his hand on his apron before holding it out to them. "If you two are anything like she is, we're glad to have you."

"I think they'll fit in alright," Jessie said, lifting her cup.

"New beginnings?" William shrugged.

"Family?" Billy added.

"How about both?" Jessie replied, clinking her cup against theirs before chugging the liquor.

"Did the mayor really offer her the marshal job right here after she shot two men in the street?" Billy asked.

Elmer smiled and nodded. "He damn sure did. She took care of the men who gunned down our marshal. She seemed like the best candidate at the time, and hasn't disappointed us yet."

William shook his head.

"What?" Jessie questioned.

"I'm not surprised. You were always two steps ahead."

"What does Bert think about having more deputies?" Elmer asked.

"He seems fine with it. It's something I've been after the mayor about for several months now."

"Well, after what happened to you last year, it seems like it took him long enough to honor your request."

"I don't think he was going to…well, not until he met these two, anyway."

"What happened to you?" Billy asked.

"She and Bert were ambushed and nearly killed, then she got shot a few months later. Almost died."

"Jessie?" William whispered, looking seriously at her.

"I told you there was some trouble here. I came out alright," she said reassuringly. "Come on, let's go get some breakfast," she added, setting some coins on the bar to pay for their drinks.

"I look forward to seeing you gentlemen again soon," Elmer said, adding, "Marshal, always a pleasure. Glad you made it home safely."

When they walked outside, William turned to Jessie. "It's definitely a lot different here."

"It's a completely different life," Jessie replied.

"No kidding."

"I like it," Billy added.

"Oh, I never said I didn't. It's just…it'll take some getting used to, is all."

"I think you boys will fit in just fine." Jessie smiled.

"Do you ever miss it?" Billy asked.

Jessie furrowed her brow. "Being an outlaw?" she questioned, then shook her head as she said, "No."

*

After breakfast, Jessie showed her brothers the rest of the small town, before making their way back to the General Trade.

"Is this place abandoned?" Billy asked, looking at the theatre.

"That's Pearl Hall, or at least it used to be," Jessie sighed. "It was a nice theatre with great shows, until a few outlaws became unruly one night. Things got out of hand when the leader of the gang tried to take one of the actresses unwillingly. He shot and killed the theatre manager in the process. The owner couldn't handle the situation, so he put it up for sale. It's been sitting empty ever since."

"What a shame," he muttered.

"Yeah, Ellie says the same thing. It definitely brought entertainment to the town. That's for sure," she said, eyeing the building solemnly as she thought about Tobias.

"Well?" Ellie said, stilling her broom as she watched the trio walk towards her.

The three of them eyed her suspiciously.

"Is it official?" she queried, placing a hand on her hip.

William and Billy proudly pulled the flap of their jackets aside, under the long, duster coats they wore to keep warm, revealing the metal badges pinned to their vests.

"Congratulations!" she exclaimed, hugging them both. "I made honey biscuits to celebrate," she added. "They're upstairs."

"Thank you," William said.

"I know we just ate, but trust me, you don't want to miss these," Jessie said. "And you had better save me two of them," she added. When they were out of earshot, she looked at Ellie. "It's pretty crowded up there, isn't it?"

"Just a little bit," Ellie laughed.

"Take a walk with me."

"I can't leave the store," she replied as Molly walked in.

"Perfect timing." Jessie grinned.

Ellie raised a brow at her wife.

"What's going on?" Molly asked.

"I want to take a walk with Ellie. Can you watch the store for a bit?"

Molly shrugged. "Sure. Eddie is still with the church ladies. I'm afraid they may want to keep him before long. I just took lunch over to Bert, and thought I'd stop in for a few things before I went to get the baby."

"We won't be gone long," Ellie said. "Thank you so much."

"It's not a bother. Take your time." Molly smiled.

"My brothers are upstairs. They've discovered the honey biscuits."

"Oh my," Molly laughed. "I still cannot get that recipe right."

"You're adding too much starch powder. I told you that last time," Ellie chided.

"Anyway," Jessie interrupted. "If they come down before we get back, tell them to go over to the Marshal's Office with Bert."

"Will do. Go on. Enjoy. I'll be right here."

"Shall we, Mrs. Henry?" Jessie asked, holding her arm out.

Ellie put on her thick shawl and placed her hand on the crook of Jessie's elbow. She flashed a smile so genuine, it made Jessie's heart flutter. Before Ellie entered her life, she'd never known what it felt like to love or be loved. It was a feeling she hoped she never lost.

NINETEEN

Many of the town folk were out and about, shuffling along the freshly shoveled sidewalks and riding wagons through the streets muddied with snow. Jessie and Ellie strolled by, waving and nodding politely to those who stopped to say hello.

"It feels so good to be back home," Ellie murmured. "Promise me you won't go traipsing across the country again."

"I don't want to be anywhere other than where you are." Jessie grinned and added, "Besides, I have no reason to ever return to Castor Valley."

Ellie looked at her. "Are you sorry you never spoke to your mother?"

Jessie shook her head. "That harlot was never a mother to me. I'd prefer it if you never mentioned her again."

Ellie saw a hint of sadness cross Jessie's face before it hardened. She sighed inwardly as they walked a little further. She missed her own mother from time to time, cursing herself for running off with Will McNally and ruining any chance at a future relationship with her family. She'd chosen him, and she'd chosen wrong, giving up everything in the wake.

"Are you looking forward to Christmas?" Jessie asked, pulling Ellie's mind out of the past. Her demeanor had softened into a playful smile.

"Sure. I always am. You know that." Ellie met her eyes. "Besides, we have family with us this year, so it will be extra special."

"I'm sorry we didn't get a proper Thanksgiving because we were traveling home."

"Don't fret. I'm sure we can make up for it at Christmas." Ellie smiled, squeezing in a little closer to her wife. The cold air was crisp and clean, and it smelled like pine. Heavy flurries began to fall once more, casually coating the sidewalk in front of them. She thought about sticking her tongue out to catch a snowflake, just as she'd done many times as a child.

"Here we are," Jessie announced.

Ellie glanced around. They were standing in front of one of the small cottage houses, which were lined in a row of four at the beginning of town. The little, white picket fence made it stand out against the others, which either had a ratty, old brown fence, or nothing at all. A skinny streak of gray smoke snaked above the chimney top. She remembered seeing it for sale and thinking how much she'd love to have a house one day. The word SOLD was painted over the For Sale sign that was stuck in the snow-covered ground, just inside the fence. "Looks like someone finally bought it," she sighed.

"Yep," her wife mumbled, pushing open the small gate.

"Jessie! We can't go in there. That's someone's house!"

"Come on," Jessie laughed, grabbing her hand and tugging her along. They walked up the two steps that led to the small front porch. Ellie looked around, hoping no one saw them, as Jessie turned the door knob.

"We could go to jail for this," Ellie hissed as Jessie pulled her inside. She took a second to look around at the expanse of the room, surprised that no one was inside. A stone fireplace was to her left with a bright orange glow from the wood burning inside. A cooking stove was to her right, with a pile of wood next to it, and a real kitchen with a counter top, a full sink, and a handful of cabinets and shelves were beside it. The kitchen sink had a window in front that looked out over the little yard and into the street beyond the fence. There was a small, open space on the other side of the stove with corner shelving. It looked as though it functioned as a dining area. The closed door that faced them was obviously the bedroom. The entire house was larger than the room above the store, with a full bedroom and kitchen, but it felt as quaint and cozy as it had looked from the outside.

Jessie watched her wife fall in love with the house, just as she had the first time she'd seen it.

"We should go," Ellie urged.

"I'm the Town Marshal and I say it's okay for a woman to want a little privacy with her wife, especially when she's barely been alone with her for over a month."

"What about the new owners?" Ellie looked at her with a confused expression.

"Do you mind if we're alone here? Because I don't."

"What?" Ellie questioned. She glanced back at the door, waiting for someone to rush in at any moment.

"Do you mind if we're alone here? I'm asking the new owner for permission to make love to her in her new house." Jessie smiled and held her hand up, cutting Ellie off when she tried to speak. "I couldn't take you looking at this house, and then talking yourself out of it, anymore. I was already in the process of buying it before I left. I even signed the papers with Mayor Montgomery in case anything happened to me, so you'd be sure to get the house. When you two showed up in Castor Valley, he informed me that everything had been finalized, and the house was ours. Early Merry Christmas!"

"Oh, my God! I love you, Jessie Henry," Ellie exclaimed, wrapping her arms around Jessie's neck, and kissing her softly. "Why are you so good to me?" she asked, leaning back to look into her eyes.

"I should ask you the same question," Jessie replied before sweeping Ellie off of her feet and carrying her into the bedroom.

*

William and Billy had moseyed over to the Marshal's Office by the time Ellie and Jessie returned to the store. They said a quick goodbye before going their separate ways. Jessie crossed the street, walking towards the Marshal's Office, and Ellie went to her shop. The bell over the door rang as she entered.

"I was wondering if you two had decided to skip town again," Molly laughed.

Realizing they'd been gone a lot longer than she'd thought, and the reason for the extended absence, made Ellie blush.

"Oh…" Molly giggled. "Do tell."

Ellie laughed. "There's not much to tell, really. Jessie surprised me with the most amazing and thoughtful early Christmas gift," she said, stopping to think about *their* little house.

"Well, let's see it." Molly looked her over, trying to make out what was different besides a few pieces of hair tucked behind her ear that had come loose from her bun, and a button on her blouse was open, which Molly pointed out.

"She bought us a house!" she blurted, unable to hide the happiness coursing through her body. She'd nearly forgotten to fix her button as she began telling Molly all about the good news.

"That's wonderful," Molly exclaimed. "Will her brothers be staying here?"

Ellie nodded. "We're going to give them the apartment upstairs."

"Sounds like a great idea. I'm really happy for you both," Molly said, hugging her friend. "I'd better go pick up Eddie before the church ladies decide to keep him. Last week, they sewed him a christening dress."

"Really? That was nice of them."

"At first I thought they did it to hurry me up because I hadn't planned it yet with Pastor Noah, but honestly, we've all been so busy as of late, there hasn't been time to even think about it. Until now, anyway."

"They can be pushy. I remember how they treated me after Corny died. They expected me to sulk around in mourning and sell the business to a man. I wore all black for nearly a year, but this store was the reason Corny and I settled here. I wasn't giving it away."

"Oh, I remember. They nearly fell over when you opened the store back up, running it yourself," Molly chuckled. "It simply wasn't the 'proper' thing to do. I thought, 'Now that's a strong woman'."

"It was more like determined." Ellie smiled. "I simply wasn't going to fail, and I definitely wasn't going to let the church ladies tell me how to live my life."

"They were fit to be tied when Pastor Noah commended you," Molly added, still laughing.

"I'm sure their archaic minds had a field day when I married Jessie."

"I never heard anything out of them. But, Pastor Noah pretty much shut down any negativity when he performed your ceremony."

"You can't fault anyone who has the church behind them," Ellie chuckled.

"I think if they could figure out how to control Pastor Noah, they'd do it."

"I'm sure they've tried."

"What's all the laughter about, ladies?" Mayor Montgomery asked, stepping inside and removing his hat.

"I'm going to go get my baby. I'll check in with you later," Molly said. "Mayor, always nice to see you."

"You as well Mrs. Boleyn."

"You get any more snow dust on my floor, I'm going to hand you a mop," Ellie chided, watching the snowflakes fall from his coat.

"I apologize," he said.

"It's fine." Ellie waved him off. "What brings you in? By the way, William and Billy are over the moon. They seemed quite proud of their badges."

"That's good. I think they'll be a fine addition. I assume everyone is settled."

"Yes, and the house is wonderful. Thank you for allowing Jessie to purchase it."

"No thanks needed. It was for sale anyhow. Plus, I'm pretty sure she swindled me," he chuckled.

"Well, she *was* a gambler at some point."

"Yes, amongst other things," he added. "Anyway, I came over to offer my congratulations on the house, and pick up a few items. It seems I ran out of certain things while I was traveling."

Ellie pinned him with an odd look. "Perhaps you have a ghost, Mayor."

He shrugged. "One who likes to be clean and drink fancy tea."

"Sounds like a woman."

He nodded in agreement. "Although, I think the spirit of my secretary is alive and well."

Ellie bit back a laugh. "Why would he borrow things from your residence to give to his wife?"

"I don't think it's his wife we're talking about."

"Well, shame on him," Ellie spat.

Mayor Montgomery laughed. "Marshal Henry sure has her hands full with you," he mumbled, remembering the headstrong woman he'd traveled with.

"I can guarantee you she doesn't have a mistress."

"Oh, I don't doubt that," he replied, grabbing a tin of peach flavored tea leaves and a jar of soap flakes. *Especially if she doesn't want to be on the wrong side of a wet hen,* he thought. "What do I owe you?"

"It's a dollar-fifty, but I can put it on your account."

"No sense in bothering," he said, placing the coins on the counter.

When he left, Ellie walked over to the door. The street was covered in a light dusting of snow, as were the sidewalks that had already been swept that morning. The snow wasn't deep enough to shovel just yet, but soon there would be piles of it everywhere.

TWENTY

Jessie found her brothers and Bert, sitting in the Marshal's Office when she entered. "What do you say we go do some target practice? I haven't seen you boys shoot a gun for over two years, and I need to make sure you haven't gone rusty on me."

"Sounds good with me," William said.

"Where did you get off to?" Billy asked.

"We'll get to that later. William, you and Billy go down to the saloon and ask Elmer for empty bottles. He'll know what you mean. Meet us back here with as many as you can carry without breaking them. You remember where it is, right?"

Her brothers nodded and headed out the door.

As soon as they were out of earshot, Jessie sat down at her desk.

"Everything okay?" Bert asked.

"Yeah," she mumbled, looking at the newspaper lying in front of her.

"That one came out while you were gone."

She scanned it quickly, then slid it into her drawer, planning to read it thoroughly later. "I'm going to alternate William and Billy on the bank stages, once they're trained, of course. Those robberies seem to be occurring more and more. It's best we have someone with ours at all times. When they're not riding shotgun, they'll be working with us around town. They need to get to know everyone, but they also need to get used to Territory Law. Thankfully, our crime rate has fallen significantly, but that doesn't mean another gang won't ride through, terrorizing the town. Besides, drunk and disorderly, and gun carry laws are something the guys aren't familiar with handling."

"That makes sense," Bert replied.

"It'll take some getting used to, for all of us. I want you to know that you're the Lead Deputy, so when I'm not here or not on duty, you're in charge. You've certainly earned it."

"I appreciate that. Thank you." He nodded.

"I'm going to have William and Billy shadow you and I for the next week, maybe a little longer. We can alternate halfway so that they get to work with each of us, learning the ropes. After that, I'll start putting them on the bank stage runs."

"That's a good idea."

"Great, now that that's all squared away, let's go have a little fun," she said with a grin.

*

Out near the tree where Jessie and Ellie got married, and Bert learned to shoot properly, Jessie set up six glass bottles in various places. Two were up in the tree, one was in bushes, two were sitting on old logs and stumps, and one more on the ground.

"How about a friendly wager," she said, spinning the magazine of her revolver before sliding her pistol back into the holster hanging from the belt around her waist.

"What are we talking?" William asked.

"We haven't been paid yet, so we got no money, Jessie."

"Then, you probably shouldn't lose, should you," she retorted with a smile. "In all seriousness, I was thinking more along the lines of the loser has to clean all the guns."

"That works for me," Bert replied, looking at the bottles.

"We have enough bottles to shoot six each. If you hit all six of your targets, you move on to the next round, until there is only one winner. The bottom two clean the guns. Deal?" Jessie said.

"Deal," the three men agreed.

"William, you're up first," Jessie announced, drawing a line in the dirt with her boot.

Everyone else took a step back as William walked to the mark. He drew his gun, then quickly aimed and shot, over and over until all six bottles busted. He holstered his pistol and moved aside for his brother as Jessie reset the targets with new bottles.

Billy moved nearly the same way his brother had, shooting all six bottles. Bert and Jessie followed suit, busting all of their bottles. Pleased that everyone had made it past the first round, Jessie grabbed the large chunks of broken bottles and began placing them once again, six at a time, but in harder places. Then, she moved back ten paces and drew a new line.

"William," she said, nodding towards the new spot.

He refilled his magazine with bullets, spun it around, then locked it in place. After a quick glance to make sure everyone was behind him, he fired his shots, again hitting all of the broken bottles.

Jessie grinned, remembering the teenage boy who could barely hold a pistol when she'd met him.

Billy, who was up next, hit all of his bottles except one. "Damn it," he mumbled.

Bert shot next, hitting all of the targets, and Jessie went behind him, also shattering all of her bottles.

"Okay, boys. This is where it gets exciting. I'm going to toss a piece of glass away from us and into the air. You have to hit three to move on," Jessie said, collecting some of the larger chards.

Bert started the round, hitting the first two and missing the last one. Billy followed, hitting only the second of three pieces. Bert tossed the glass for Jessie and William, who both made all of their shots.

"You boys aren't as rusty as I thought you'd be." She smiled. "Billy, you get to clean all of the guns."

"I'll help him. I missed a target, too," Bert added.

"That's fine. You can show him where everything is. I have a stop to make. You can clean mine when I get back," she replied, heading away from them as they turned towards town.

*

Billy was just about finished with the guns, and Bert was showing William some of the log books they used to keep up with ammo and other supplies, when Jessie appeared, holding an array of beautiful, freshly-picked wildflowers.

"Here," she said, handing Billy her pistol.

"You're still using this thing?" he smiled.

"Hasn't failed me yet," she replied, hurrying off.

Both of her brothers watched her scurry across the street with a huge smile on her face.

"She's never let anyone else touch that thing, much less take it apart to clean it," Bert muttered, looking at the pistol in Billy's hand.

He shrugged. "I always lost the shooting game when we ran together, so I'm used to doing the cleaning. It's messy, but not that big of a deal," he replied, setting it down on the canvas sack that was used to cover Bert's desk.

At that same moment, Ellie had escorted a customer to the door, hoping to catch a glimpse of her wife, out keeping the streets safe.

All three men saw Ellie's face light up when Jessie handed her the flowers. She sniffed them before throwing her arms around Jessie's neck, and kissing her cheek. They stood casually for a second, laughing and talking, then disappeared inside.

William and Billy looked at each other with odd expressions. Neither of them had ever seen Jessie affectionate towards anyone.

"I'll be damned," William mumbled, surprised to see how in love Jessie and Ellie really were.

"I don't think I've ever seen Jessie smile so much," Billy said as he went back to the silver pistol with ivory grips, and began disassembling it.

Bert thought about when he'd first met Jessie and how hardnosed she was back then. She was still tough as nails, but Ellie had certainly softened her rigid edges since they'd been together.

*

Ellie walked down the spiral staircase with a vase full of water. She arranged the flowers the way she wanted them, then stuck them inside.

"They're beautiful," she said, smiling at Jessie.

"I would've taken them to the house, but I know we don't have anything there yet."

"Speaking of that," Ellie said, "I was planning on packing as soon as I close the store today. We need to figure out furniture."

"Let's get through Christmas. It's only a few weeks away. After that, we can have some stuff built."

Ellie nodded. "I'd love a dining table to put in that nook area. At least we have a bed there. Do you think we can start sleeping at the house tonight?"

"Sure. I don't plan on being crammed into that room upstairs anymore. Besides, our new bed is pretty comfortable." Jessie grinned, causing Ellie to blush.

"We don't have a whole lot of things to move. I plan on leaving as much behind for your brothers as I can. Obviously, I'm going to take most of my cooking stuff though."

"That's a good idea. I can't let the boys go out on their own for a week or so. After that, they'll be on their own. I'll have more time to help you with getting the house set up then."

"What did they say about it?"

"I haven't told them."

"Why not?" Ellie asked, adjusting the flowers before setting the vase behind the register where all of her customers would see it.

"It hasn't come up. I'm going to go tell them now, though. I decided to bring those to you first," she said, nodding towards the flowers.

"You keep spoiling me, Jessie Henry, and I may never let you stop," she teased, kissing her cheek.

"I figured you'd be used to it by now." Jessie shrugged. "Bert was definitely right. I should've listened to him a lot sooner."

"What do you mean?"

"He kept telling me to take you flowers. I thought he was a fool."

"A fool who is happily married, so he must've done something right."

"Yeah," Jessie laughed. "He took her flowers!"

Ellie chuckled and shook her head as Jessie walked out of the store.

*

As she made her way back across the slushy street, Jessie thought about the house once more. The chill in the air was getting worse, and the clouds threatened another snowfall before the end of the day. She wondered if there was enough wood for the fireplace to last all night. She was in such a haste to show the place to Ellie, she'd lit it and then went to get her.

"What's wrong?" Bert asked, noticing the grimace on Jessie's face as she stepped inside, brushing the snow dust from her shoulders and hat.

"Just thinking about something," she said, holstering her freshly cleaned gun when Billy handed it to her. "Let's take a walk."

"Me?" Billy questioned, looking oddly at her.

"All of us."

The boys glanced at Bert, who simply shrugged and followed her. The four of them walked together down the sidewalk along Main Street. When the path ended, Jessie led them along the street towards the row of houses that sat on the edge of town, just inside the town limit. She stopped in front of the one with the short, white, picket fence.

"What do you think?" Jessie asked, holding her arms out.

The three men stared at her like she'd sprouted antlers.

"This is mine and Ellie's house," she added.

"What? How?" Billy questioned.

"Since when?" Bert asked.

"I started the deal to buy it before I left, and it finalized while I was gone. I signed the papers this morning. It's ours."

"Wow. The Old Rayburn Place. This is great," Bert said.

"William and Billy, we're giving you the room above the store, free for a month. Then, we'll come up with some kind of rent, but it's yours as long as you want it."

"Are you sure?" William asked.

"Absolutely."

"We'll take it," Billy exclaimed.

"Great. Now that that's all settled, let me show you the house." Jessie led the way, showing them around the small house. She made note that there was plenty of chopped wood next to the stone hearth.

"You've done alright for yourself," William said, lighting a cigar as they stood on the front porch. "I was worried at first, but you've made a good life for yourself out here."

"I think you and Billy will, too. It's a lot different than outlawing on the frontier, that's for sure." She smiled, also lighting a smoke. "Are you two done? It's not that big," she called inside, waiting for Bert and Billy to come out of the house.

"I like it," Billy said.

"Molly is going to want a new dining area as soon as she sees this," Bert mumbled.

Jessie laughed. Recalling the open space, gave her an idea.

TWENTY-ONE

The next three weeks went by in a blur. Ellie was quite busy with town folk buying holiday gifts, and dry goods to prepare their Christmas dinners. Jessie and Bert were showing her brothers the ropes, which pretty much consisted of walking the snow-covered streets, freezing, and drinking coffee with a splash of whiskey to keep warm.

*

"I can't believe it's Christmas Eve," Ellie said, her voice cheerful with happiness. She threw open the curtains at the front of the house, allowing the little bit of afternoon sunlight peeking through the snow clouds to fill the room. Then, she glanced around at the open space behind her and frowned. A small Christmas tree stood in the corner of the room, with shreds of red ribbon and white lace wrapped haphazardly around it, and a tiny angel carved out of wood on the top. "I do wish we had furniture though," she sighed.

"All in good time," Jessie replied, sneaking up and wrapping her arms around Ellie's waist. "It takes a while to make furniture. And with the holidays, it's nearly impossible to find anyone that can do it."

Ellie looked at the rickety pair of chairs sitting by the fireplace. Jessie could do a lot of things, but she wasn't much of a carpenter, which showed in the chairs she and her brothers threw together, with Bert's help. They looked as if they may crumble at any moment, but they were still holding up.

"I told William and Billy to swing by the stable and pick up the hay bales I ordered. At least we'll have something for people to sit on." She shrugged.

"I have a couple of quilts I can throw over them."

"See." Jessie grinned, adding, "It's coming together already," as she moved aside to put more logs on the fire.

Ellie laughed and shook her head. She started to turn away from the window, when she saw a covered wagon stop in front of their house. "What in the world?" she mumbled.

Jessie smiled and ran to get her overcoat.

"Who is that?"

"William and Billy."

"How many hay bales are they bringing?" she croaked.

Jessie shrugged. "I told them to go pick up my order," she called over her shoulder as she headed outside.

Ellie checked the pot of apple cider and a kettle full of tea leaves on the stove, making sure they were heated perfectly before removing them.

"I need you to go wait in the bedroom, please," Jessie said, stepping back into the house.

"What on earth for?" Ellie questioned with her hands on her slender hips. "What's so exciting about hay bales?"

"It seems they've brought a surprise for you, and me, but I promised not to peek as I unload our new seating arrangement."

"Jessie Henry, I believe you're trying to put me on."

"Nonsense. Why would I fool my own wife?"

Ellie grumbled as she went into the bedroom and shut the door.

*

"You didn't tell us it would be this heavy," William blurted, as he helped Jessie unload the wagon.

"Just pull your breeches up and keep moving before she comes out," Jessie growled through her teeth. "Hurry up Billy," she hissed, waiting for her brother to set the last piece of heavy wood in place, which made a thud sound on the floor.

"Is everything okay?" Ellie called. "I'm coming out." The smell of fresh cut pine filled her nose.

Jessie rushed to stand between her brothers, over near the dining nook.

"Oh my!" Ellie squealed, noticing the brand new, firmly built chairs in front of the fireplace, replacing the wobbly ones which seemed to have disappeared. A small, matching table sat between them. "They're perfect!" she added, sitting down in one of the chairs. "Is all of this from you, boys?"

"No," they said in unison.

"I got it for you," Jessie said. "To go with this," she added as she and her brothers moved aside, revealing the round dining table and four chairs, all made of the same wood as the other furniture pieces. "Merry Christmas, Ellie."

"Good heavens!" Ellie cried, rushing into her arms. "Its…I love it all. And I love you." She leaned back, kissing Jessie's soft lips.

"I love you, too."

"I still can't believe you had all of this made. We've barely been in the house."

"Ike, the stable hand at the livery, built everything. His cousin owns the lumber mill over in Pinewood, so he gets the wood for next to nothing. He did a great job on Bert's desk, and has built furniture for some of the town folk. He's thinking of starting a furniture business in town."

"I think that's a splendid idea," Ellie replied, moving to sit in one of the dining chairs. She ran her hand over the smooth table top. "This is…beautiful," she murmured.

"It's not so bad over here either," William said.

"Nope," Billy agreed.

The two men were sitting in the chairs by the fireplace with their legs stretched out. Jessie glanced at the floor, noticing the bearskin rug for the first time. "Where did that come from?"

"What?" Ellie asked, standing to peer around her wife.

"Us," they said together, grinning from ear to ear. "Merry Christmas!"

Ellie and Jessie walked over, bending down to run their hands over the soft fur.

"I love it!" Ellie exclaimed, hugging them both.

"I'm speechless," Jessie murmured.

"We didn't have a whole lot of money, beings how we just started working and all, but we wanted to do something nice for the two of you."

"I'm sorry we couldn't save the head," Billy said. "I shot him in it."

Ellie raised her eyebrows and giggled. "It's fine. I'm glad you didn't add the paws either. It looks less animal-like this way."

Jessie turned it over, taking a look at the finishing. "You boys did a great job. It's perfect right here," she said, hugging them.

"Since we're giving gifts," Ellie mumbled, turning away from the group to walk over to the tree. "Here you go," she continued, handing a paper-wrapped package to each of the men.

"You didn't have to get us anything," William said.

"Of course we did, you are our family," Ellie stated, urging him to open his gift.

Billy unwrapped a red-paisley, ascot-style tie and matching handkerchief. "This is fancy," he uttered, holding it up to his chest. "Thank you!"

Ellie nodded and smiled.

William was also given a new tie, but his was a black ribbon bow-tie. "I like it. Thank you," he said, somewhat unsure how to wear it.

"I figured you were more like her, black, black, black," Ellie said, referring to Jessie's lack of color in her wardrobe.

"You were right," he laughed.

The boys brought two of the dining chairs over to the fireplace area and sat down as Ellie went into the bedroom. She came back out a minute later with another paper-wrapped package, but this one was a little larger.

"Did you think I'd forgotten you?" Ellie teased, seeing the look on Jessie's face as she handed it to her.

"No." Jessie shook her head. "I found this days ago."

"Oh, you sneak!" Ellie exclaimed, smacking her playfully on the arm.

"Not on purpose," Jessie chuckled. "I dropped my sock and when I bent down to get it, I saw something under the bed."

Ellie crossed her arms and turned her nose up, pretending to be mad.

Jessie grinned as she tore open the thick paper, revealing a new white shirt and a pair of silver cufflinks with JH etched in them.

"Wow," she whispered, holding the small, metal pieces between her fingers.

"I knew you'd bought a new suit a few months back, but the tailor hadn't had any shirts in your size. I asked to make sure you hadn't come back for one later on. When he said no, but he'd made one just in case, I took it."

"Clever girl." Jessie grinned.

"Do you like the cufflinks?"

"They're perfect. I love them, and I love you," Jessie said, smiling brightly as she wrapped Ellie in her arms, kissing her tenderly on the lips.

Ellie kissed her back before remembering their guests and clearing her throat. Jessie turned to see her brothers looking shyly at the floor like young boys, witnessing a loving moment between their parents.

"William, Billy, would either of you like a cup of warm apple cider or tea? I used leaves soaked in honey," Ellie called, walking into the kitchen.

William asked for tea, and Billy opted for cider.

Everyone settled on chairs in front of the fire, with Billy and William sitting in the chairs they'd brought over from the dining set.

"What were the holidays like when you were all together?" Ellie asked.

"You mean when we were outlawing?" Billy said.

Ellie nodded.

Jessie set down the cup of cider she was casually sipping. "You don't want to hear stories about those days. There's certainly nothing exciting about what we did."

"It wasn't all that bad," Billy uttered. "We had a lot of fun together during the good times. All outlaws have three things in common: booze, gambling, and women. We definitely had our fair share of all three, especially when the money was rolling in, but that life for us, was a lot more than just those things. We were free to do whatever we wanted. There were no rules. No laws. Just us, our horses, and our campsite. We spent more times than I'll ever remember, watching the most beautiful sunrises and sunsets a man could ever see in one lifetime, and staring up at a sky so full of stars, they look like they're all connected together."

William thought for a moment. "We weren't settled anywhere, and moved our campsite quite often. Animal skins gave us something to sleep on besides the hard dirt. Luckily, it doesn't rain much in the desert, so wet weather wasn't much of a problem. We weren't rich, not by any means. Most of our money came from holdups or was stolen from other gangs we rounded up for the bounty, which we also got paid on. Some of it came from crooked gambling. We had to be careful with spending, so we didn't bring unwanted attention to ourselves. It definitely wasn't any kind of life like this," he said, looking around the room. "But, we cared for each other, and watched each other's back like a family. Living that life, you don't really have a sense of what day it is, but you can usually tell the month by the weather and the changing of the seasons. We never had proper holidays, at least not after Billy and I lost our mother."

"I never had any to begin with," Jessie added. "I think that's why the three of us were so good together. We didn't care much about holidays and birthdays, and settling down. We did what we wanted. We bought ourselves things when we needed or wanted to. We even ate at restaurants and attended a theatre show or two, if we were unknown and in a new place." She stared at the flames of the fire, then sighed, "But we were always on the run, and always looking over our shoulders, no matter where we went."

"What were the holidays like for you?" Billy asked, looking at Ellie.

Jessie hadn't said anything to her brothers about Ellie's ex-husbands or the McNally Gang. She'd told her that her past was her story to tell, and she never had to repeat it again if she didn't want to.

After a long sip of honey tea, Ellie looked out the window. Heavy snowflakes were falling outside. "Holidays at home were always large gatherings of people in our house. My sister and I were our parents only children, so we were doted on. She was daddy's girl, and momma and I were the best of friends, at least we were," she sighed. "I married young and ran off unknowingly with a scoundrel, turning away from my family. He was killed a couple of years later, but by that time, it was too late to go home. I traveled around and settled here with my second husband. We fell in love with the town and opened the store together. Our first holidays here were some of the best I'd ever had. Pearl Hall, the theatre that's now closed, used to hold these lavish Christmas Eve parties. Most of the town would go, and everyone was dressed in their best clothing. We would dance the night right into morning. Those were such happy times, despite the ruckus the gangs were causing around town. I wish you could've seen Pearl Hall at its best," she said to Jessie. "The theatre closed over two years ago, and the town hasn't been the same. The gangs are gone, thanks to Jessie and Bert, but a light went out when they closed the doors. It's quite sad really. I'm sure a lot of town folk miss those times. Anyway, those were some of my best holidays, but now I'm making new ones." She smiled.

"What happened to your second husband?" Billy asked.

"He heard a fight outside of our store in the middle of the day and being the sincere person he was, he went outside to help break it up. He was shot, and died right there in the street. I loved him, but I've never loved anyone the way I love your sister," she said, catching Jessie's green eyes as they locked onto her.

"She hated me at first," Jessie laughed.

"Oh, did I ever," Ellie chuckled. "I wanted to swat her with the broom!"

Both men guffawed.

"What did she do?" Billy questioned.

"She was arrogant and demanding, and I couldn't concentrate when she was around. She knew it and used it against me."

Jessie grinned and shrugged. "It worked, didn't it?"

"Of course. I fell head over heels in love with you." Ellie smiled again and squeezed her wife's hand.

Billy and William gave each other a subtle nod. Something about being around Jessie again, and seeing her with Ellie, made them feel like they were finally home.

"We should probably get out of your hair and let you two enjoy your new furniture. Thank you again for the gifts," William said.

"You don't have to run off," Ellie said.

"Actually, we need to get the wagon back. The stable hand let us borrow it to deliver the furniture," Billy replied.

"Make sure you're here tomorrow at noon for Christmas Dinner," Ellie informed. "And be careful out in the snow. It's coming down in heaps."

Jessie pulled her overcoat on and walked her brothers outside. "She's right. You two be careful. You're not used to riding in this."

"We'll be fine. You go have a nice evening, and we'll see you tomorrow," William said.

"The old days don't compare to the life we all have now. This is the best holiday I've ever had," she uttered.

"Me too," Billy agreed, hugging her.

"Yeah," William mumbled and nodded, also hugging her.

Jessie watched the boys climb up into the seat, brush away the snow, and trot off, waving back to her. Turning towards the house, she saw Ellie standing near the window. She smiled and rushed back in, shaking the white flakes from her coat and hat before hanging them on the rack by the door.

*

Later that evening, after a simple brisket and potato dinner, the two women were settled into their new chairs in front of the fireplace. Bright flames licked the stone walls of the hearth, casting the room in a warm, orange glow.

"I really do love these chairs, and that table is stunning. Wait until Molly sees it," Ellie stated.

"Bert's still trying to figure out how to build a dining nook in their house."

"I know," Ellie laughed. "Poor thing."

Jessie removed her tie, laying it on the table. Then, she removed her new cufflinks, placing them next to the tie, and rolled the sleeves of her shirt back a little bit. "What's that under the tree?" she said.

"What?" Ellie glanced over in the corner.

"Did you forget something?"

"No," Ellie said curiously as she walked over to retrieve it. "Did you get something else for your brothers?"

Jessie shook her head. "Maybe it's for you."

"Me?" Ellie questioned, opening the box. A beautiful pair of turquoise and silver earrings glistened in the dim light. "Oh, my word!"

"Do you like them?" Jessie asked, standing up from her chair.

"Absolutely," she cooed, removing them from the box. She slid one into a hole in each ear, and let them dangle. "How do they look?"

"Better than I ever could've imagined," Jessie said, kissing her softly. "Will you dance with me?" she asked, stepping back and holding her hand out.

"With no music?"

"Sure. Why not?" Jessie grinned.

Ellie's heart pounded in her chest. She loved the way Jessie looked at her, like nothing else in the world existed. She put her hand in Jessie's and let herself be pulled into position. She put her other hand up on Jessie's shoulder, and Jessie's arm slid around her waist.

Jessie couldn't remember the last time she'd danced, but listening to Ellie's story about Pearl Hall made her want to spin Ellie around the floor. She hummed a tune and concentrated on each step as they moved together in the middle of the room. *One, two, three. One, two, three. Turn. One, two, three.*

"You're a fine dancer, Marshal Henry," Ellie said softly.

"You as well, Mrs. Henry," Jessie replied, turning her once more.

They glided around dancing as if they'd been doing it for years, laughing and smiling, and stealing tiny kisses here and there. When they finally came to a stop, Jessie pulled her watch from her vest pocket and flipped it open. It was 12:01AM.

"Merry Christmas," she exclaimed, putting it away and moving closer, running the back of her fingers down the delicate skin of Ellie's cheek as she stared into her eyes.

"I know a way to make it even merrier," Ellie said, grabbing her hand and pulling her down to the fur rug.

THE END

About the Author

Graysen Morgen is the bestselling author of *Falling Snow*, *Fast Pitch*, *Cypress Lake*, *Meant to Be*, *Coming Home*, the Never Series: *Never Let Go* and *Never Quit*, the Bridal Series: *Bridesmaid of Honor*, *Brides*, and *Mommies*, as well as many other titles. She was born and raised in North Florida with winding rivers and waterways at her back door, as well as, the white sandy beach. She has spent most of her lifetime in the sun and on the water. She enjoys reading, writing, fishing, coaching and watching soccer, and spending as much time as possible with her wife and their daughter.

You can contact Graysen at graysenmorgen@aol.com; like her fan page on Facebook.com/graysenmorgen; follow her on Twitter: @graysenmorgen and Instagram: @graysenmorgen

Other Titles Available From
Triplicity Publishing

Close Enough to Touch by Cade Brogan. Joanna Grey injects the deadly poison into the chamber of the syringe—time after time. She's murdered before and she'll do it again. She's intelligent, educated, and beautiful. Rylee Hayes is a respected homicide detective. Her best friends are her grandparents, her coonhound, and her partner—in that order. Kenzie Bigham is the single mom of a thirteen-year-old, a church secretary, and a woman who's struggled much of her adult life with her own sexuality. Their paths will cross when Rylee's new investigation involves members of Kenzie's congregation. Will Rylee have what it takes to meet the challenge of a serial killer who's proven herself to be a more than worthy opponent?

Fight to the Top by S. L. Gape. Georgia is a forty year old, single, Area Director from Manchester, UK who is all work and definitely no play. Having no time to socialise or spend time with her family she prides herself on being fit and well-polished. Erika is an Area Director for the same company, but in the United States. Whilst she is concentrating so heavily on the promotion she has been fighting for, she's starting to feel like her life outside of work is falling apart. The two women are exceptionally different, and worlds apart. Both of their lives are turned upside down when their jobs are snatched from under their noses, and they are suddenly faced with being thrown together by their bosses for one last major project...in Texas.

Boone Creek (Law & Order Series book 1) by Graysen Morgen. Jessie Henry is looking for a new life. She's unknown in the town of Boone Creek when she arrives, and wants to keep it that way. When she's offered the job of Town Marshal, she takes it, believing that protecting others and upholding the law is the penance for her past. Ellie Fray is a widowed, shopkeeper. She generally keeps to herself, but the mysterious new Town Marshal both intrigues and infuriates her. She believes the last thing the town needs is someone stirring up trouble with the outlaws who have taken over.

Witness by Joan L. Anderson. Becca and Kate have lived together for eight years, and have always spent their vacation in a tropical paradise, lying on a beach. This year, Becca wanted to try something different: a seven day, 65-mile hike in the beautiful Cascade Mountains of Washington state. Their peaceful vacation turns to horror when they stumble upon a brutal murder taking place in the back country.

Too Soon by S.L. Gape. Brooke is a twenty-nine year old detective from Oxford, who has her life pretty much planned out until her boss and partner of nine years, Maria, tells her their relationship is over. When Brooke finds out the truth, that Maria cheated on her with their best friend Paula, she decides to get her life back on track by getting away for six weeks in Anglesey, North Wales. Chloe, a thirty three year old artist and art director, owns a log cabin on Anglesey where she spends each weekend painting and surfing. After returning from a surf, she stumbles upon the somewhat uptight and enigmatic Brooke.

Blue Ice Landing by KA Moll. Coy is a beautiful blonde with a southern accent and a successful practice as a physician assistant. She has a comfortable home, good friends, and a loving family. She's also a widow, carrying a burden of responsibility for her wife's untimely death. Coby is a woman with secrets. She's estranged from her family, a recovering alcoholic, and alone because she's convinced that she's unlovable. When she loses her job as a heavy equipment operator, she'll accept one that'll force her to step way outside her comfort zone. When Coy quits her job to accept a position in Antarctica, her path will cross with Coby's. Their attraction to one another will be immediate, and despite their differences, it won't be long before they fall in love. But for these two, with all their baggage, will love be enough?

Never Quit (Never Series book 2) by Graysen Morgen. Two years after stepping away from the action as a Coast Guard Rescue Swimmer to become an instructor, Finley finds herself in charge of the most difficult class of cadets she's ever faced, while also juggling the taxing demands of having a home life with her partner Nicole, and their fifteen year old daughter. Jordy Ross gave up everything, dropping out of college, and leaving her family behind, to join the Coast Guard and become a rescue swimmer cadet. The extreme training tests her fitness level, pushing her mentally and physically further than she's ever been in her life, but it's the aggressive competition between her and another female cadet that proves to be the most challenging.

For a Moment's Indiscretion by KA Moll. With ten years of marriage under their belt, Zane and Jaina are coasting. The little things they used to do for one another have fallen by the wayside. They've gotten busy with life. They've forgotten to nurture their love and relationship. Even soul mates can stumble on hard times and have marital difficulties. Enter Amelia, a new faculty member in Jaina's building. She's new in town, young, and very pretty. When an argument with Zane causes Jaina to storm out angry, she reaches out to Amelia. Of course, she seizes the opportunity. And for a moment of indiscretion, Jaina could lose everything.

Never Let Go (Never Series book 1) by Graysen Morgen. For Coast Guard Rescue Swimmer, Finley Morris, life is good. She loves her job, is well respected by her peers, and has been given an opportunity to take her career to the next level. The only thing missing is the love of her life, who walked out, taking their daughter with her, seven years earlier. When Finley gets a call from her ex, saying their teenage daughter is coming to spend the summer with her, she's floored. While spending more time with her daughter, whom she doesn't get to see often, and learning to be a full-time parent, Finley quickly realizes she has not, and will never, let go of what is important.

Pursuit by Joan L. Anderson. Claire is a workaholic attorney who flies to Paris to lick her wounds after being dumped by her girlfriend of seventeen years. On the plane she chats with the young woman sitting next to her, and when they land the woman is inexplicably detained in Customs. Claire is surprised when she later runs into the woman in the city. They agree to meet for breakfast the next morning, but when the woman doesn't show up Claire goes to her hotel and makes a horrifying discovery. She soon finds herself ensnared in a web of intrigue and international terrorism, becoming the target of a high stakes game of cat and mouse through the streets of Paris.

Wrecked by Sydney Canyon. To most people, the *Duchess* is a myth formed by old pirates tales, but to Reid Cavanaugh, a Caribbean island bum and one of the best divers and treasure hunters in the world, it's a real, seventeenth century pirate ship—the holy grail of underwater treasure hunting. Reid uses the same cunning tactics she always has before setting out to find the lost ship. However, she is forced to bring her business partner's daughter along as collateral this time because he doesn't trust her. Neither woman is thrilled, but being cooped up on a small dive boat for days, forces them to get know each other quickly.

Arson by Austen Thorne. Madison Drake is a detective for the Stetson Beach Police Department. The last thing she wants to do is show a new detective the ropes, especially when a fire investigation becomes arson to cover up a murder. Madison butts heads with Tara, her trainee, deals with sarcasm from Nic, her ex-girlfriend who is a patrol officer, and finds calm in the chaos of police work with Jamie, her best friend who is the county medical examiner. Arson is the first of many in a series of novella episodes surrounding the fictional Stetson Beach Police Department and Detective Madison Drake.

Change of Heart by KA Moll. Courtney Holloman is a woman at the top of her game. She's successful, wealthy, and a highly sought after Washington lobbyist. She has money, her job, booze, and nothing else. In quiet moments, against her will, her mind drifts back to her days in high school and to all that she gave up. Jack Camdon is a complex woman, and yet not at all. She is also a woman who has never moved beyond the sudden and unexplained departure of her high school sweetheart, her lover, and her soul mate. When circumstances bring Courtney back to town two decades later, their paths will cross. Will it be too late?

Mommies (Bridal Series book 3) by Graysen Morgen. Britton and her wife Daphne have been married for a year and a half and are happy with their life, until Britton's mother hounds her to find out why her sister Bridget hasn't decided to have children yet. This prompts Daphne to bring up the big subject of having kids of their own with Britton. Britton hadn't really thought much about having kids, but her love for Daphne makes her see life and their future together in a whole new way when they decide to become mommies.

***Haunting Love* by K.A. Moll.** Anna Crestwood was raised in the strict beliefs of a religious sect nestled in the foothills of the Smoky Mountains. She's a lesbian with a ton of baggage—fearful, guilty, and alone. Very few things would compel her to leave the familiar. The job offer of a lifetime is one of them. Gabe Garst is a police officer. She's also a powerful medium. Her work with juvenile delinquents and ghosts is all that keeps her going. Inside she's dead, certain that her capacity to love is buried six feet under. Anna and Gabe's paths cross. Their attraction is immediate, but they hold back until all hope seems lost.

Rapture & Rogue by Sydney Canyon. Taren Rauley is happy and in a good relationship, until the one person she thought she'd never see again comes back into her life. She struggles to keep the past from colliding with the present as old feelings she thought were dead and gone, begin to haunt her. In college, Gianna Revisi was a mastermind, ring-leading, crime boss. Now, she has a great life and spends her time running Rapture and Rogue, the two establishments she built from the ground up. The last person she ever expects to see walk into one of them, is the girl who walked out on her, breaking her heart five years ago.

Second Chance by Sydney Canyon. After an attack on her convoy, Marine Corps Staff Sergeant, Darien Hollister, must learn to live without her sight. When an experimental procedure allows her to see again, Darien is torn, knowing someone had to die in order for this to happen.

She embarks on a journey to personally thank the donor's family, but is too stunned to tell them the truth. Mixed emotions stir inside of her as she slowly gets to the know the people that feel like so much more than strangers to her. When the truth finally comes out, Darien walks away, taking the second chance that she's been given to go back to the only life she's ever known, but she's not the only one with a second chance at life.

Meant to Be by Graysen Morgen. Brandt is about to walk down the aisle with her girlfriend, when an unexpected chain of events turns her world upside down, causing her to question the last three years of her life. A chance encounter sparks a mix of rage and excitement that she has never felt before. Summer is living life and following her dreams, all the while, harboring a huge secret that could ruin her career. She believes that some things are better kept in the dark, until she has her third run-in with a woman she had hoped to never see again, and gives into temptation. Brandt and Summer start believing everything happens for a reason as they learn the true meaning of meant to be.

Coming Home by Graysen Morgen. After tragedy derails TJ Abernathy's life, she packs up her three year old son and heads back to Pennsylvania to live with her grandmother on the family farm. TJ picks back up where she left off eight years earlier, tending to the fruit and nut tree orchard, while learning her grandmother's secret trade. Soon, TJ's high school sweetheart and the same girl who broke her heart, comes back into her life, threatening to steal it away once again. As the weeks turn into months and tragedy strikes again, TJ realizes coming home was the best thing she could've ever done.

Special Assignment by Austen Thorne. Secret Service Agent Parker Meeks has her hands full when she gets her new assignment, protecting a Congressman's teenage daughter, who has had threats made on her life and been whisked away to a Christian boarding school under an alias to finish out her senior year. Parker is fine with the assignment, until she finds out she has to go undercover as a Canon Priest. The last thing Parker expects to find is a beautiful, art history teacher, who is intrigued by her in more ways than one.

Miracle at Christmas by Sydney Canyon. A Modern Twist on the Classic Scrooge Story. Dylan is a power-hungry lawyer who pushed away everything good in her life to become the best defense attorney in the, often winning the worst cases and keeping anyone with enough money out of jail. She's visited on Christmas Eve by her deceased law partner, who threatens her with a life in hell like his own, if she doesn't change her path. During the course of the night, she is taken on a journey through her past, present, and future with three very different spirits.

Bella Vita by Sydney Canyon. Brady is the First Officer of the crew on the Bella Vita, a luxury charter yacht in the Caribbean. She enjoys the laidback island lifestyle, and is accustomed to high profile guests, but when a U.S. Senator charters the yacht as a gift to his beautiful twin daughters who have just graduated from college and a few of their friends, she literally has her hands full.

Brides (Bridal Series book 2) by Graysen Morgen. Britton Prescott is dating the love of her life, Daphne Attwood, after a few tumultuous events that happened to unravel at her sister's wedding reception, seven months earlier. She's happy with the way things are, but immense pressure from her family and friends to take the next step, nearly sends her back to the single life. The idea of a long engagement and simple wedding are thrown out the window, as both families take over, rushing Britton and Daphne to the altar in a matter of weeks.

Cypress Lake by Graysen Morgen. The small town of Cypress Lake is rocked when one murder after another happens. Dani Ricketts, the Chief Deputy for the Cypress Lake Sheriff's Office, realizes the murders are linked. She's surprised when the girl that broke her heart in high school has not only returned home, but she's also Dani's only suspect. Kristen Malone has come back to Cypress Lake to put the past behind her so that she can move on with her life. Seeing Dani Ricketts again throws her off-guard, nearly derailing her plans to finally rid herself and her family of Cypress Lake.

Crashing Waves by Graysen Morgen. After a tragic accident, Pro Surfer, Rory Eden, spends her days hiding in the surf and snowboard manufacturing company that she built from the ground up, while living her life as a shell of the person that she once was. Rory's world is turned upside down when a young surfer pursues her, asking for the one thing she can't do. Adler Troy and Dr. Cason Macauley from Graysen Morgen's bestselling novel: *Falling Snow*, make an appearance in this romantic adventure about life, love, and letting go.

Bridesmaid of Honor (Bridal Series book 1) by Graysen Morgen. Britton Prescott's best friend is getting married and she's the maid of honor. As if that isn't enough to deal with, Britton's sister announces she's getting married in the same month and her maid of honor is her best friend Daphne, the same woman who has tormented Britton for years. Britton has to suck it up and play nice, instead of scratching her eyes out, because she and Daphne are in both weddings. Everyone is counting on them to behave like adults.

Falling Snow by Graysen Morgen. Dr. Cason Macauley, a high-speed trauma surgeon from Denver meets Adler Troy, a professional snowboarder and sparks fly. The last thing Cason wants is a relationship and Adler doesn't realize what's right in front of her until it's gone, but will it be too late?

Fate vs. Destiny by Graysen Morgen. Logan Greer devotes her life to investigating plane crashes for the National Transportation Safety Board. Brooke McCabe is an investigator with the Federal Aviation Association who literally flies by the seat of her pants. When Logan gets tangled in head games with both women will she choose fate or destiny?

Just Me by Graysen Morgen. Wild child Ian Wiley has to grow up and take the reins of the hundred year old family business when tragedy strikes. Cassidy Harland is a little surprised that she came within an inch of picking up a gorgeous stranger in a bar and is shocked to find out that stranger is the new head of her company.

Love Loss Revenge by Graysen Morgen. Rian Casey is an FBI Agent working the biggest case of her career and madly in love with her girlfriend. Her world is turned upside when tragedy strikes. Heartbroken, she tries to rebuild her life. When she discovers the truth behind what really happened that awful night she decides justice isn't good enough, and vows revenge on everyone involved.

Natural Instinct by Graysen Morgen. Chandler Scott is a Marine Biologist who keeps her private life private. Corey Joslen is intrigued by Chandler from the moment she meets her. Chandler is forced to finally open her life up to Corey. It backfires in Corey's face and sends her running. Will either woman learn to trust her natural instinct?

Secluded Heart by Graysen Morgen. Chase Leery is an overworked cardiac surgeon with a group of best friends that have an opinion and a reason for everything. When she meets a new artist named Remy Sheridan at her best friend's art gallery she is captivated by the reclusive woman. When Chase finds out why Remy is so sheltered will she put her career on the line to help her or is it too difficult to love someone with a secluded heart?

In Love, at War by Graysen Morgen. Charley Hayes is in the Army Air Force and stationed at Ford Island in Pearl Harbor. She is the commanding officer of her own female-only service squadron and doing the one thing she loves most, repairing airplanes. Life is good for Charley, until the day she finds herself falling in love while fighting for her life as her country is thrown haphazardly into World War II. Can she survive being in love and at war?

Fast Pitch by Graysen Morgen. Graham Cahill is a senior in college and the catcher and captain of the softball team. Despite being an all-star pitcher, Bailey Michaels is young and arrogant. Graham and Bailey are forced to get to know each other off the field in order to learn to work together on the field. Will the extra time pay off or will it drive a nail through the team?

Submerged by Graysen Morgen. Assistant District Attorney Layne Carmichael had no idea that the sexy woman she took home from a local bar for a one night stand would turn out to be someone she would be prosecuting months later. Scooter is a Naval Officer on a submarine who changes women like she changes uniforms. When she is accused of a heinous crime she is shocked to see her latest conquest sitting across from her as the prosecuting attorney.

Vow of Solitude by Austen Thorne. Detective Jordan Denali is in a fight for her life against the ghosts from her past and a Serial Killer taunting her with his every move. She lives a life of solitude and plans to keep it that way. When Callie Marceau, a curious Medical Examiner, decides she wants in on the biggest case of her career, as well as, Jordan's life, Jordan is powerless to stop her.

Igniting Temptation by Sydney Canyon. Mackenzie Trotter is the Head of Pediatrics at the local hospital. Her life takes a rather unexpected turn when she meets a flirtatious, beautiful fire fighter. Both women soon discover it doesn't take much to ignite temptation.

One Night by Sydney Canyon. While on a business trip, Caylen Jarrett spends an amazing night with a beautiful stripper. Months later, she is shocked and confused when that same woman re-enters her life. The fact that this stranger could destroy her career doesn't bother her. C.J. is more terrified of the feelings this woman stirs in her. Could she have fallen in love in one night and not even known it?

Fine by Sydney Canyon. Collin Anderson hides behind a façade, pretending everything is fine. Her workaholic wife and best friend are both oblivious as she goes on an emotional journey, battling a potentially hereditary disease that her mother has been diagnosed with. The only person who knows what is really going on, is Collin's doctor. The same doctor, who is an acquaintance that she's always been attracted to, and who has a partner of her own.

Shadow's Eyes by Sydney Canyon. Tyler McCain is the owner of a large ranch that breeds and sells different types of horses. She isn't exactly thrilled when a Hollywood movie producer shows up wanting to film his latest movie on her property. Reegan Delsol is an up and coming actress who has everything going for her when she lands the lead role in a new film, but there one small problem that could blow the entire picture.

Light Reading: A Collection of Novellas by Sydney Canyon. Four of Sydney Canyon's novellas together in one book, including the bestsellers Shadow's Eyes and One Night.

Visit us at www.tri-pub.com